INTERROGATIONS

By A.J. Brown

Interrogations

Disclaimer: *Interrogations* is a work of fiction. Names and events are creations from the author's imagination, except where noted.

Edited by Larissa Bennett and Donelle Pardee Whiting
Proofed by Tara Bennett
Cover art and layout by Lisa Vasquez

Print First Edition, 2019

Dedicated to my kids, Chloe and Logan. I couldn't have asked for better children than you two. I love y'all.

Interrogations
(A Hank Walker Story)

It had been a long time since he had seen his face without a bush of hair on it. It had been a long time since his hair had been cut, this chore done by an older black gentleman. His name was Mr. Johnson, and he once owned a barbershop before the end of the world. Though the room smelled strongly of aftershave and shaving lotion, there was an underlying scent tickling Hank's nose. It wasn't quite musky, but there was something strong and sharp to it. He couldn't quite place the smell, but it was there the entire time Mr. Johnson cut his hair and told his stories.

"I cut hair on the same corner for fifty-three years before all this happened," Mr. Johnson said proudly as he cut away inch after inch of the long locks on Hank's head. "Started out on the sidewalk, cutting for a quarter here or there and whatever tips I might could get. Wasn't much to be had most days, but I still did my best. Eventually some folks came back and … I'm sorry. I must be boring you to tears, young man."

"No, not at all, Mr. Johnson. Go ahead. I'd like to hear your story."

Hear the story? Hank smiled at his own words, not really believing he had said them. But wasn't it the truth? Everyone had a story to tell. Some told it easily enough; others would probably never mention theirs. They were more like the war veterans he had known as a kid—those from World War II and Vietnam. They didn't talk about the horrors they had seen. For them, it was too hard. He figured most people straddled the fence somewhere in the middle, willing to talk about their lives before the biters, reminiscing for what it was worth, and then after the biters, commiserating with those seeking solace and comfort. He gathered he was one of them, maybe not sharing in the misery, but the memories.

Mr. Johnson continued his story, his voice carrying the sound of a man who had suffered more than his fair share of loss, ending it after he placed a hot rag on Hank's neck and the words, "But I'll take anyone I can get right now. Cutting hair has always been therapeutic. You know?"

"Yeah, I know." He didn't.

"All done there, Mr. Walker."

2

A mirror appeared in front of Hank. When he looked in it, he saw another mirror being held behind his head.

"It looks nice, Mr. Johnson," he said, not lying this time. "I appreciate it, sir."

He hadn't thought much about getting his hair cut, but the old man offered, and he had taken him up on it. He got a shave out of the deal as well. Looking in the mirror in the school's bathroom half an hour later, he realized he had forgotten what he looked like and wasn't so sure he liked what he saw. The man he had seen in Mr. Johnson's quarters had been foreign to him. The man who stared back at him was vaguely familiar, as if he recognized him, but couldn't place a name to him.

"You look like Lee," he whispered as he leaned into the mirror, his hands clutched tight on the sink. It was true. He squeezed the sides of the porcelain sink, afraid if he let go he might fall. Tears spilled down his cleanly shaved face, but he couldn't look away; couldn't pull his hands free from the sink.

"Little bro, promise me you won't let me get like that. Promise me you'll put me down before I die."

Lee's words echoed in his ears.

Lee died, and I couldn't put him down right away and he woke … as one of them. I should have put the bullet in his head way before then, but I couldn't. I just … couldn't.

Hank saw Lee's head move and then lift. His eyes fluttered open, and the top of his head exploded as the bullet hit home. Hank's jaws clenched, and without so much as a real thought, he released the sink and swung his right fist at the mirror. It shattered on contact. Slivers of glass fell into the sink and onto the floor, while other pieces stuck into his bloody, wounded knuckles. Hank lowered his fist. The mirror had been only a flat wall piece, probably hung there when the high school was built, way before it was turned into Fort Survivor South Carolina Number Three.

Blood dripped from his hand as he left the bathroom and went down the hall to his quarters. There, he took a towel from a box on the floor and wrapped his hand. It only took a couple of minutes for the blood to seep through, soaking it red.

That had been this morning, before Hetch came into his quarters, saw the bloodied towel, and taken Hank down to the nurse's office, which was only a room inside what used to be the school's

Administrative Office—the place the principal, vice principal, counselors, and office staff worked.

Now it was early afternoon, and he sat in a faded green plastic school chair, one so many kids sat in during better days, even if they didn't know things were great for them then. How many of those kids were in there for disciplinary reasons?

Most of them, he thought.

But he was pretty certain none of them had to sit across from a principal resembling the man in front of him. This guy didn't wear a nice shirt and tie and studious glasses on the bridge of his nose, and he didn't talk in tones meant to intimidate a kid; though, Hank thought he could—and would—if necessary. He was an older guy—not a gentleman by any shade of the imagination. What little hair he had was white and buzzed tight to his skull. His skin was like tanned leather, and his cold green eyes could make most men piss their pants. But he didn't look as mean as Hank thought he could be. No, this man was never a principal. If Hank had to guess, he was a man who fought in a war or two and killed a bunch of the enemy. He looked like a general, and one who was good at his job.

The only thing separating the two men was the large desk the General sat behind. The desk itself wasn't remarkable at all. It had four corners that came to points and a black desk blotter on the top. On top of it was a yellow notepad, a pen, and a clear glass filled with water.

And there was that scent. It smelled older in there. Hank wasn't sure, but maybe his senses were on hyper drive. After being out in the world with the dead for so long, maybe his sense of smell was trying hard to catch something which wasn't rotting. And it wasn't like the aroma of the dead. It was stronger and appealing, but something he thought could drive him crazy after a while.

"How are you, Mr. Walker?" he asked. His voice wasn't gruff, but smooth and comforting. He could be easy to talk to.

He must have been a shrink in the old world.

"Alive," Hank said.

The General nodded, gave a slight chuckle. "This you are," he said and motioned to Hank's lap. "What happened to your hand?"

Hank lifted it and stared at the blood-stained bandage Doctor Andrews had placed over the wound. She had been nice, too. Nichole, that's what she said her name was. Young, pretty, and somehow a survivor like the rest of them in the compound. Like Mr. Johnson's chambers, the nurse's office had an odor which permeated through the sterile smell. It wasn't as strong, but it was still there. She had stitched the wounds, apologizing with each poke and pull of the needle and thread.

"No need to apologize," Hank finally said. "I've been through a lot worse."

Her lips didn't quite form a smile—Hank wasn't sure she was able to do that yet—but there was something in the slight upturn of one side of her mouth. "Haven't we all?" she responded.

"I reckon so."

She finished sewing the hand, picking out slivers of mirror as she did so. Leaving, he got the beck and call from the General, who'd been standing outside the nurse's door like a pissed off principal. And in the room Hank smelled a scent. It was heady, like the thick smell of cigars, but there was something else in it, something he couldn't quite place.

"Can I ask you something, first?"

The General frowned but didn't say 'no.' "Sure. Go ahead."

"What's your name?"

The General's frown deepened, then gave way to a broad smile. If he didn't know better, Hank would swear the man blushed in embarrassment, but this guy, this man was not a blusher and didn't embarrass easily. "I guess that would be good for you to know, wouldn't it?"

"Yeah, especially since we're in the principal's office, and this doesn't strike me as a strictly friendly get to know you type of thing."

"Fair enough," the General said and then offered his name. "My name is Harrison Avis, and I run Fort Survivor South Carolina Number Three. It's my job to keep these people safe, and we've done a pretty good job of that since we arrived here."

"How long ago was that?"

"Almost five months ago."

"Five months? That's a long time."

"Yeah. You should have seen this place before we arrived, before we cleaned it out and built it up."

"I can imagine."

Hank knew the guy's name now, but he wasn't so sure he trusted him. Or if Harrison Avis trusted Hank.

"So, Mr. Walker, do you mind me asking what happened to your hand?"

Images flashed in his mind: the mirror, his brother's last few minutes, death and subsequent rising, and the bullet that ended his suffering, forever Hank hoped.

"I punched one of the mirrors in the bathroom."

"Why did you do that?"

"Remembering."

Avis's eyebrows rose. "Remembering what?"

"My brother, Lee."

"What about him?"

Hank didn't look at Avis. He stared down toward the corner of the desk. It held a scuff mark on it, where someone either kicked it out of anger or fear, or maybe someone shoved the very chair he sat in against it when they left.

A student maybe?

Yeah, a student. One like Lee, who could get in trouble just by walking into a room. He would have sat in the chair Hank was in more times than the rest of the Walker brothers combined. Practical jokes and smart remarks toward the teachers happened on a regular basis when they were in school. But back then, the principal would bend you over and make you grab the arms of a wooden chair and tell you to "hold on tight, boy, you're going for a ride." Then came the whack of the wooden paddle on the hind side. It was always a jarring thing, getting hit by the paddle and not being able to really move. Standing up straight or letting go of the chair always warranted one extra smack.

"Mr. Walker?"

Hank shook his head, all thoughts of Lee and school and spankings fading. "Yeah?"

"Are you okay?"

"Yeah." He nodded but didn't believe he was. Avis didn't appear to believe him either. His lips cut a straight line across his face, and his eyes weren't quite squinting, but they had narrowed considerably. "Just … just … ummm … thinking."

"About what?"

"My brother."

"The same one you were thinking about when you broke the window in the bathroom?"

"Yeah."

10

"I'm going to guess he's dead."

"Yup."

Hank wanted to get up, say "thanks for the chat," and get out of there. He wasn't so sure he wanted to be in the office or the building or his chambers, which was still in an isolated unit, one far away from Jake and Bobby, and even Hetch. But he didn't think it was a good idea. Though Avis seemed like an okay guy, there was something there, an underlying temperament that didn't sit well with Hank. Or maybe it was the fact he was around so many living people it unnerved him. Except for Hetch, every other living person he met during the End Times, as he heard a couple of people refer to it, had been crazy or almost there.

"Do you want to tell me about it?"

"Not particularly."

"Mr. Walker, if you ever want out of Quarantine, then you're going to have to cooperate with me."

"I am cooperating. You asked if I wanted to tell you what happened to my brother. I said, no. That's cooperating."

"Are you certain?"

"Mr. Avis, is this an interrogation?"

11

"It doesn't have to be."

"Are *you* certain?"

"It's an information gathering, Mr. Walker."

"You want to make sure I'm sane, is that it?"

"Pretty much."

"What if I'm not?"

Avis grinned, just enough to be there and show no humor at all. "That's not something you want, Mr. Walker."

Hank didn't respond, he knew Avis was right. The alternative to being safe was one of two things: get sent back outside the compound's walls, or death by a bullet or some other means to the head.

"What do you want to know?"

"Ready to cooperate?"

"If that's what will keep me with my son, then yes."

"It's the only thing that will accomplish that."

Hank sat in the uncomfortable chair, his hands on his lap, his feet directly in front of him and planted on the floor. Nerves danced along the edges of his skin. His jaw clenched, unclenched, and clenched again. When he realized he was doing this, Hank tried to relax, but failed. He was the bad kid Lee had always been. He sat in front of the principal waiting to tell his side of the story, hoping he would believe him. If not, it was "bend over and grab your ankles, son, this is going to hurt."

"Why don't we start from the beginning," Avis said and picked up the pen. He licked the tip, something Hank hadn't seen anyone do since he was a kid, and it was what Pop always did before writing a check. It made the tip of the pen wet, allowing the ink to flow easier if the pen had been sitting for a while. But Pop didn't care—the pen could have been brand new, and he would have licked it anyway. *Force of habit,* Hank thought.

"What's your name?"

"Hank Walker."

"Your full name?" Avis said, looking up from the pad.

"Henry Thomas Walker."

"Where did you live before the End Times?"

"The End Times? That's what everyone is calling this?"

Of course, it is, you heard it yourself, Hank old boy.

"Yes."

"I hardly think it's the end times, Mr. Avis. If it were, then all of us would probably be like the biters on the other side of the wall out there."

"Then what would you call it, Mr. Walker?"

"Hell."

"Maybe it is, Mr. Walker. And maybe we missed the boat during the rapture, and all of the dead are soulless husks the devil has possessed, and they're going to wipe out the rest of mankind. If that's the case, Mr. Walker, then I guess we'd all be sinners."

"According to the Bible," Hank said, "we're all sinners anyway."

Avis sat quiet for less time than it seemed. Finally, he spoke, his words clipped and sharp, almost daring Hank to argue with him. "I guess that just depends on your religious beliefs, Mr. Walker. Do you have religion?"

Hank thought of his mother. She had religion right to the very end, but she died before the End Times. And, if her religion was true, then she's somewhere better and probably waiting with Pop and Lee and Rick and the rest of the family for Jake and Hank and Bobby to come home.

"Honestly, I don't know anymore."

Mom would be disappointed.

14

"So, then you had religion at one point, and now you don't?"

"I don't think that really matters much for this conversation; do you, Mr. Avis?"

The small smile came back, and Avis nodded. "Of course not." He tapped his fingers on his desk. "Where did you live before The End Times?"

"A little town called Sipping Creek. Most folks have no clue where it's at."

"How long were you out there?"

"Out where? In Sipping Creek?"

"No. Out *there*." Avis pointed toward the door with his pen, indicating beyond the walls.

"From the beginning?"

"I think you know what I mean."

"You asked a simple question, Mr. Avis. I gave you the only answer I know. I was out there from the very beginning. If that's not good enough, then I don't know what is."

Silence followed, then was broken. "Were you alone?"

"Mostly."

More snapshots, images danced in his head for a moment and were gone: Pop, Davey Blaylock, Lee, the crazy preacher and his flock of Chosen Ones,

15

the two rednecks on the side of the road, the old man feeding his dead wife the living, Imeko and what was left of his people, Hetch. There were other things, other people, most of them dead, he guessed, and all of them only there for a few moments; moments which felt like someone else's life.

"Mostly?"

"In the beginning there were four of us. My brother, my best friend, and my dad. They all died over a three-day span five weeks in. Then there was Hetch. I guess we were together for a couple months. Time doesn't really exist out there."

"Tell me about them."

"No."

"Excuse me?"

"I won't tell you about them or what happened. Those memories will stay locked in my head."

"It's good to get them off your chest, Mr. Walker."

"I don't need to get them off my chest."

"It's good for the soul."

"Not mine."

"Well, then it could be good for your heart. If you talk about them and get it all out of your system, you will feel better."

"I don't feel bad. Not right now."

"You must have earlier, or you wouldn't have punched a mirror. Sometimes talking about your memories helps them go away."

"I don't want them to go away. I want to remember. Remembering keeps me alive."

"Mr. Walker …"

Hank let out a deep breath, rolled his eyes, and shook his head. Avis was persistent and a bit annoying. If he wasn't a head shrink before, he probably should have been. Then again, if he was half annoying back then, he may not have had many patients. The thought of him being a shrink gave him an idea—bargaining chip, maybe.

"I tell you what, a story for a story."

"I don't understand." From the down turned lips and brows, and the slightly squinted eyes, Hank had a feeling—an intuition, if you will—Avis was lying.

"You want to know what happened out there, right? I'll tell you, but for each story I tell you, you have to tell me one about what you saw out there. Who you lost. What do you say?"

"Mr. Walker, this isn't about me. It's about you and whether I think you are safe to be around the people here."

"You want to know about me?"

"I do."

"I want to know about you in return. Like a relationship. It's give and take. I'll give, but you have to give as well. A story for a story. That's the deal."

Avis shook his head. His lips formed a thin line across his face. His nostrils flared like a bull about to charge. "No deal, Mr. Walker." His voice was decidedly deeper.

"Then my memories remain mine."

Again, there was silence.

"Mr. Walker … ummm … Hank. Can I call you Hank?"

"No." He heard the edge in his own voice. It's something he doubted he would have heard before, but this isn't before, and this isn't the old Hank Walker.

"Mr. Walker, maybe we got off on the wrong foot here."

"Maybe. Can I ask you something?"

"I think we need to get back to you, Mr. Walker."

Avoidance. Hank knew the tactic well. He had seen many coworkers and supposed friends do it when asked direct questions. Usually, the avoidance was met with lies.

He's hiding something.

"Can we get back to the information gathering, Mr. Walker?"

"By all means."

Sitting across from the man he first thought was a general, and one intent on dragging the wrong type of information from him, made Hank remember what he didn't like about people in the old world. Everyone had an agenda, as did Harrison Avis. And maybe Avis had a good reason for his agenda, but Hank didn't like not knowing more about him other than his name. How about a rank and what branch of the armed forces he served in? Would that be too much?

"What did you do before the End Times?"

"I worked in a warehouse."

"A warehouse?"

"That's what I said."

Avis raised one eyebrow. There was a glint of something not so nice there, and then it was gone. Hank didn't wait for the next question.

"What about you?"

"I told you. This isn't about me."

Hank chuckled. It was a simple thing, and one he tended to do when aggravated.

"What's so funny?"

"Nothing, really. It's just you said this wasn't an interrogation, but you're acting like it is. You want to know about me, about what happened out there, if I'm safe to be around people, and you don't even want to talk. Just talk. You know, like a couple of guys at a bar, drinking beers. That's what my brothers and I used to do. Sit at a table at a bar and act like we were watching football, but really all of our entertainment came from talking about our lives, our wives, our jobs, our kids."

Hank leaned forward, put his elbows on the too-clean desk, folded his arms at the wrist, and looked into the cold eyes of Harrison Avis. "I don't like interrogations. I get what you're trying to do and all, but you're going about it the wrong way. What you should have done is put me at ease, a little small talk. But, you're not like that are you? Is that

20

what the 'End Time' did to you? Take away your small talk?"

"Mr. Walker, I hardly think—"

"Maybe you should try it, Mr. Avis."

Avis cocked his head to the side, then straightened it. His eyes had narrowed, and his lips were a thick line across his face. He stared hard at Hank, as if trying to intimidate him.

"Mr. Walker, I've about had enough of you."

"I've about had enough of you, too, so we're even."

"Are you going to answer any of my questions without an argument?"

Hank said nothing at first, pondering the question and his answer. Finally, he said, "I'll answer your questions if you answer just one of mine."

Avis seemed to think it over, looking down at his pad and tapping his pen on it. When he looked up his lips were pursed. He licked them, nodded once and then spoke, "One question. That's all you get."

Hank almost smiled but held back. "Okay. One question it is."

"So, what's your question?"

"How long were you out there? Among the dead?"

Avis didn't answer. He didn't look away from Hank, but he swallowed hard. His eyes narrowed again, an act Hank suspected Avis didn't realize had happened.

"It's a simple question. How long were you out there before you got here?"

Avis licked his lips again. He swallowed hard again.

Hank leaned further on the desk, his chest touching it. "You *were* out there at some point, right?"

Avis stared at Hank, his eyes like hot embers on an open flame. Hank's eyes grew wide, and he knew the truth, even if Avis didn't want to speak it.

"You weren't, were you?"

Avis's nostrils flared, his lips puckered, and his eyes narrowed to full squints. "No, I wasn't."

Hank stood.

"Sit down, Mr. Walker."

"No."

"Mr. Walker—"

"I'm not the dangerous one here. You are."

"How do you figure?"

"You haven't been face-to-face with the biters. You haven't seen people torn apart by them. You didn't bury your loved ones after putting a bullet in their heads. I'm not dangerous. I understand surviving out there—"

"If not for your friend and my men, you would be dead, Mr. Walker."

"Maybe so, but I lasted what, eight months out there? You wouldn't have lasted that long, would you? At least your soldiers know what it's like, at least they have been there, seen it, and lived it."

"Mr. Walker, I answered your question, now sit down."

"No. You didn't answer the question. I figured it out. But why don't you answer this one—how many people have you put out of here? How many people have you sent back out there because *you* thought they were dangerous? How many people did you send to their deaths without having a real clue what it's like to be out there?"

"Mr. Walker, sit down." Avis spoke through clenched teeth.

"When you struggle for food and water, shelter and safety, and fight for your life, you come talk to

23

me. When you see one of your loved ones die, literally, right in front of you, come get me. When you see them open their eyes after they've died and get up and try to eat you, come find me. We'll have us a beer and a talk and pretend we're watching football. When you've cried at your wife's grave and have the soul crushing guilt of her death on your head, then I'll sit down and answer your questions. Hell, I bet your family is still all alive, aren't they?"

Avis said nothing again, only glared at Hank with full anger on his face.

"Yeah, that's what I thought. I tell you what, when you step outside those walls with one of them and face the real horrors and the dead all around you, come get me. I'll listen to you tell me how you survived, and I'll tell you how I did. Until then, have a good day."

"Mr. Walker ..."

Hank turned back. "One other thing, if this is who you are now and you haven't been out there," this time Hank pointed toward the door for the same affect Avis went for earlier, "then this is probably who you were before the End Times.

Because being out there changes people. And you … it would have changed you for certain."

"How's that, Mr. Walker? How would it have changed me?"

"It would have changed you from the living to the dead. You would be one of them."

Hank left Avis sitting at his desk. He thought he would regret it later, be outed or even executed for not cooperating or showing no respect to the man in charge. The time wasn't now. Now Hank walked away, through the office and passed the stunned staff working at desks which used to belong to others, people who were more than likely very dead. He half expected Avis to come after him, to try and stop him and detain him if he could. Yeah, detain was the right word.

He was out the main office doors, and no one had said anything. Though he thought maybe Avis would go after him, he didn't think the guy would physically try to restrain him, even if he was ex-military or a former cop or whatever it was he did before the End Times. And if he did, weak or not, Hank would have no problems fighting the guy. If anything, to have someone who had never been on the outside, face to face with the biters, question him and try to gauge whether he was safe or not, pissed him off almost beyond the two rednecks outside Batesburg.

As he made his way up the hall, his hands clenched into tight fists, he felt heat on his face and neck. A pulsing sensation hummed behind his eyes. His jaw flexed and released and … and there was something else. Something nagged at him, and as he passed someone in the hall he realized what it was.

Hank slowed as he and the man approached each other. He was older, easily in his seventies. He walked with a limp and was slightly hunched over. His hair was white, but not neatly combed. There were liver spots on his hand and one on the side of his face.

"How do?" the old man asked as he drew near Hank.

"I'm fine," Hank responded, but he didn't think he sounded fine. "How about you?"

"Better in here than out there, son."

Hank gave a nod. "I hear you."

The man limped on, not giving Hank a second look. Hank however, stopped and watched the man go. He wore loose khakis and a light blue button-down shirt. But that wasn't what made him stare after the old man. Hank inhaled, and his mind woke fully to the thing nagging at him.

I smell him.

It was a startling thought and made him pause for a moment. He recalled the sweet scent of the nurse, the rustic scent of the barber, and the cigar stench of Avis. And now came the aroma of the old man. It was rustic like the barber's but was mixed with a medicinal lotion sunk deep into his muscles. What made it worse was the sound filling his ears for just a second. It was the old man's heartbeat, a slow, but steady thumping.

The man rounded the corner, but Hank lingered a second or two longer. He sniffed the air, much like an animal would. The old man's scent was faint but still there. Hank shook his head, a frown creasing his face.

"That was weird," he whispered, as he turned and walked away.

He entered the room he had been assigned, closing the door behind him.

"D'you see the mirror in the bathroom?"

Hetch sat in a yellow plastic chair, one leg on the other knee, a book in his hand. Hank looked at him in time to see him slip a piece of paper between the pages and close the book.

"Yeah."

"How'd the mirror get broken?"

"What are you reading?" Hank asked instead of answering the question.

"Your life story, Hank. Now, how'd the mirror in the bathroom get broken?"

Hank held his hand up. The splotch of red had spread on the bandage around the knuckles.

"You hit it?"

Hank shrugged. "I guess so."

"Why?"

"Memories have a way of haunting a person, you know?"

A nod and Hetch said, "Yeah, I do."

"I reckon so." Hank eased himself onto the bed he woke in. It wasn't necessarily comfortable, but it beat lying dead in some girl's bedroom with a shotgun blast to the head. He kicked his legs up and leaned back, placing his hands behind his head. At least the pillow was soft. He stared at the ceiling—nothing more than the simple drop variety with black specks throughout. How many pencils had been tossed up there, getting stuck for a few seconds before gravity had its way and plucked it free? He remembered doing it in detention a couple of times after the crazy Mr. Carney left the room.

"So, where have you been all morning? I've been waiting for a while."

"I got called to the principal's office."

Hetch cocked his head to the side. One side of his mouth turned up in an odd smile, more curious than anything else.

"Avis had some questions for me."

"Oh, you had to deal with him? Not the friendliest guy in the world."

"Nope. I don't like him."

"Already making enemies?"

"If that's what you want to call it, then sure."

"What would you call it?"

"Seeing through his BS."

Hetch's brows lifted. "What do you mean?"

"He likes having power."

"You think?"

"He's dangerous, Hetch. I would watch what I say around him."

"Why do you say that?"

"Did you have to talk to him?"

29

"I think everyone does."

Hank nodded and sat up in the bed. "Did you mention getting bit?"

Hetch hesitated, looked down at the floor and then back up at Hank.

"I didn't think so."

"Hank, it's not what you think."

"What do I think?"

"You think I didn't tell them because they might kick me out or—"

"Or try to bash your head in?" Hank finished for him.

"Yeah."

"I think you're right."

"Did he ask you about being bitten?"

"We didn't get that far."

In short order Hank relayed the conversation to Hetch. When he finished, he said, "I don't trust him as far as I can throw him."

Hetch shook his head slowly, his eyes down to the white tiled floor. "So, he's never been out there? He's never had to fight for his life?"

"Nope. Never. And I don't trust anyone who hasn't witnessed it firsthand."

"I can't believe that."

"Believe it, Hetch. Avis is dangerous, maybe even more so than a handful of biters."

Silence filled the room. Hank stood from the bed, stretched, though he didn't need to. "So, what did you want?"

Hetch looked up at him, his eyes coming back from a distant stare into nothing. "What?"

"You said you have been here for a while. What did you want?"

"Oh, ummm … I was just seeing what you were up to. That's all."

"Really? That's it?"

"Yeah, that's it."

"You're a lousy liar."

"That's never been one of my strong suits."

"Ain't that the truth? So, what did you want?"

Hetch frowned. Again, he looked down at his feet. When he looked back at Hank, he seemed tired, he seemed *older*. "I was worried, Hank. I wanted to make sure you were okay. We almost lost you, and well, I didn't want to lose another friend."

"Friend?" Hank asked. "Who said we were friends?"

Hetch frowned. Hank saw the confusion in it.

"I'm kidding, Hetch."

His body sagged in what Hank took as relief. "You had me going there, man. That's a good one."

"Have you seen Bobby?"

Hetch stood. "He's in the gym. He came by earlier looking for you. I told him when I saw you I would let you know where he was."

"Well, where is he?"

"What? You didn't hear me? I said he is in the gym, shooting hoops with some of the other kids."

Shooting hoops? With other kids? Hank thought on this for a second. Shooting hoops with other kids. He never thought he would hear something like it ever again, but he had, and one of those kids shooting hoops was his son. *How cool is that?* he asked himself.

"Do you know where the gym is?" Hank asked.

"I sure do."

The gym was on the other side of the school, separated by a dozen classrooms turned into housing, and the cafeteria, which was a little more than a quarter of the bottom floor. It only took a few minutes to get there, and when he reached the opened double doors he heard the distinct sounds of sneakers squeaking on hardwood, basketballs being dribbled and clanging off the rims. Every few seconds he would hear the *SWISH* of a ball going through the net.

Nothing but net, they would say as kids

There was laughter, and someone yelled "game point."

They walked inside. It was almost as he imagined. The floor was hardwood, the emblem of a wildcat at the half court line. There were four sets of goals, one in each corner of the gym. There were two more goals, but they were lifted into the rafters—the game time goals. Bleachers sat on both long sides of the court, each one with several folks sitting on them, watching their children or friends play.

Bobby was on the far court, furthest from the door they entered. He shot the ball, missed it, and went for his own rebound. He turned and tossed the ball to another kid, this one a girl with long, dark hair.

She's cute, Hank thought and sat on the bottom row of bleachers. He turned to say something to Hetch, but he was gone. It was okay. He wanted to be alone anyway, at least until Bobby was done playing, then he wanted to spend time with his son.

Like the nurse and the old barber, and Avis and the old man in the hall, he could smell all those around him. The scent of their sweat wasn't quite overpowering, but it rolled off their bodies in great waves. Hank put a hand over his nose, trying to be discreet about it. His stomach rumbled and his mouth watered. The smell of the sweaty kids and the dry aroma of those not playing mixed together, forming a nauseating odor that didn't quite make him gag, but close.

He didn't know how long he sat there, watching not only his son and the awkward flirtations going on between him and the young lady, but he watched the other kids as well. He counted them, sometimes getting thirty-five kids, while other times getting thirty-four.

Close enough, he thought.

Not all of them played basketball. Quite a few just shot baskets and talked, maybe feeling each other out, seeing who was safe in their minds. He wondered what all they had been through, who had seen their parents or other loved ones torn apart by the biters. Who had just barely escaped while losing everyone they loved? He thought he could figure it out easily enough. The ones not playing and sitting by themselves, their eyes off in the land of remembrance. Those kids had seen some things that left deep scars, ones which may eventually lead to opting out when no one else was around.

Hank looked over to where Bobby and the little girl had been. They were no longer shooting. They were no longer even on the court. The ball Bobby had been playing with was now in the hands of a couple other boys. Hank looked around. *Where did they go?* He started to stand, then stopped when he heard Bobby's voice.

"Dad? What are you doing here?" He had come from the other direction. With him was the dark-haired girl. From a distance, she had been cute, from up close she was pretty, with big green eyes and a perky nose above her thin lips.

Uh oh, he thought. *You've been busted spying on your kid.*

"I just stopped by to watch you play for a little while."

"Dad, I don't play. I just shoot around." Red blossoms appeared on his cheeks.

"Well, I just wanted to see you."

Bobby smiled. He was every bit Jeanette's son, and he could see so much of her in him. His heart ached, and a cloud seemed to move in over his emotions.

"We're going to the library for a little while. Is that okay?"

Hank gave a nod. "Sure. You two run along and have fun."

"Okay, Dad. I'll see you in a little bit."

They turned and went toward the door. Hank's heart sank a little further. He would have liked a hug from his son. A kiss on the cheek would have been nice, but the boy had a girl with him, so he could rule it out. But a hug …

"Hey, Bobby," he called.

They both turned around.

"I love you, son."

He thought Bobby would turn even redder than earlier with embarrassment or make a mean face at him. Instead, Bobby smiled and said, "I love you, too, Dad." He waved and both he and the girl— one Bobby had not bothered to introduce him to— were gone from the gym.

Hank sat on the bleachers a little while longer, his thoughts on his son.

How is he not ruined? How is he okay? He saw his mother get killed. He …

He was alive. Though Jeanette had died, Bobby was alive. He had survived somehow. He and Jake. Tears touched the corners of his eyes. He wiped them away and looked around the gym at the kids playing, parents watching. The world went on, even if the dead didn't stay that way anymore.

It was then he noticed the overbearing smell of the place again. It wasn't the smell of the dead he had gotten so used to while out there, but the rich aroma of the living, complete with sweat and excitement coursing through their bodies and along their skin.

One young boy walked by him, sweat dripping. Hank took a deep breath and caught the scent of game induced adrenaline. From the way the boy smiled, they had won the game.

Hank's stomach rumbled and his mouth watered. His breathing suddenly increased. He wiped his mouth with the back of one hand.

Another kid walked by him, slowed, and then stopped. "Hey, mister, are you okay?"

37

Like the other kid, this one was soaked in sweat, but the adrenaline had ebbed. Hank could smell him, too. He could smell the concern pouring off the boy. He could smell the fear.

"I'm fine," Hank said and stood. "I'm just not feeling all that well."

"You should go see the nurse. She can get you feeling real good, if you know what I mean."

Hank did know, but he wondered how the kid would. Then again, the kid probably knew more than Hank. Kids always seemed to be more in tune with what went on around the world than their older counterparts.

He had been to the nurse once already. Maybe going back would be a good idea. Maybe she could explain to him why he smelled the things he did or why he suddenly broke out into sweats. Or she could report him to Avis.

'Hey, Mr. Dictator, sir, this man is sick with the rots. We need to throw him out the gates and soon.'

He didn't think she would turn him in for something as simple as a case of the sweats and a sense of smell clogged with the aroma of the dead over the last year. But he didn't know her well, either. Who knew what she would do?

Hank had also gotten a good whiff of the sweet aroma spilling off her skin. If he lingered long enough near her, the scent would probably be intoxicating. He shook his head at the thought. The boy still stood near him, but a few feet away. His ball was tucked under one arm and he leaned over to look at Hank.

"You sure you're okay, man? You don't look so good."

Hank came all the way back from his thoughts. The boy looked more scared than concerned.

"Yeah, I'm okay," Hank said and stood. "Have a good day, kid."

With that he left the gym, going back the way he came.

He was suddenly tired. His legs were weak and his chest was tight. He turned down a hallway leading to the stairs. When he saw there was no one around, he stopped, put one hand on the wall, and took several deep breaths.

What's going on?

His head spun and his mouth grew dry. His vision grayed along the edges, increasingly swallowing up the world around him. Hank pinched the side of his face, bringing fresh pain that pushed the gray back to the edges. Another pinch and the gray subsided completely. His stomach knotted, but at least he wasn't on the verge of passing out. Another deep breath and he let go of the wall. Though he was unsteady for a few more seconds, he thought he could make it to his room.

I hope.

And he did. It took him longer than he thought it would, and his legs didn't want to work quite right, but he made it, trying not to attract any attention, but not sure he succeeded. He was certain a few people gave him wary glances, and maybe even squeezed themselves closer to the wall when he passed.

When he reached his room, he collapsed onto his bed, rolled onto his side, and pulled the blanket over his shoulder. He was asleep in seconds.

It was afternoon when he woke. His stomach grumbled, and his head was in a fog. The room was gray, the shades—the old roll down type his grandmother used to have on her windows—were still down. There was a sliver of light from the ends of those shades. With the little bit of light in the room, he could see the white ceiling and walls, and they seemed to be moving with an in-and-out rhythm.

The room is breathing …

And it did so right along with him. With the breathing was the heartbeat, a steady *th-thump, th-thump* cadence. Hank sat up and shook his head. He rubbed his eyes with the heels of his hands and took several deep breaths. The room's steady in-and-out, in-and-out rhythm made his head spin and his stomach cramp.

Hank stood on shaky legs and took two steps before gravity took hold, and he fell. He saw the floor grow close, but there was nothing he could do, no way to stop and cushion the landing. He barely had time to get one hand out in front of him to lessen the impact. A jarring pain rippled up from his left hand all the way into his elbow and shoulder. The arm taking the brunt of the fall collapsed on him, and he landed on his chest.

He laid there for several minutes, the world still spinning, the room still breathing.

"What's going on?" His voice was raspy and didn't sound like it came from him. He looked toward the door expecting to see someone there, but it was shut, though he could see the hall lights shining through the thin window he forgot to cover before crawling into bed.

He got his hands beneath him and pushed up. His arms shook, but he managed to get to his knees. In front of him was the door, behind him his bed.

"I'm not going out there," he whispered and slowly crawled back to the bed. It took him several long seconds to pull himself to his feet using the foot of the bed to aid him. Then he fell back onto the mattress and lay there, staring at the turning ceiling. He closed his eyes, but the world continued to spin.

Eventually, sleep pulled him into her arms, and he dreamed.

Hank ran along a road. It was a familiar dirt and rock road, houses to his right and left. He knew the lake was nearby, and he also knew he should have been running through the back yards by the lake and not the road. Still, it was the road he ran on and he could see the little girl off in the distance being chased, not by nameless biters, but by Davey Blaylock, and Lee, Rick, and Pop, and Jeanette, Karen, and Jessica and her kids. They were all biters, their bodies rotting away even as they ran, their arms extended, their mouths snapping. They were gaining on her.

She screamed for help. She screamed in fear. And then her head snapped back, blood spraying from the hole in her forehead. Unlike when it happened, in this dream world, the dead didn't slow down to dine on the girl, they continued running, passing her and approaching Hank.

But there was something wrong with this scene. The dead weren't groaning or growling. They were yelling and there were words on their voices and …

Hank woke and the room was dark. No light came through the curtained window, but there was a beam of white coming through the window in the door. At first he thought he was still dreaming. Muffled noises came from somewhere. The noises sounded like people yelling or screaming.

"Am I still asleep?"

His voice sounded real in his ears. Then he pinched his arm and winced with the needle-like pain that faded almost as soon as he felt it.

"I'm awake."

But he still heard the yells and screams. He sat up slowly, afraid his world would start turning again if he moved too fast. But his world didn't spin. His stomach didn't roll. He didn't feel sick at all. But the yells …

Hank swung his feet out of the bed and tested his legs before trying to walk. When he was certain they would hold him, he went to the door. As he did so, the yelling grew louder. He opened the door, and the dream was gone, and the shouts he heard were real. He had a sudden urge to go for his pistol, but he didn't have it. He didn't have any of his weapons.

Because I'm dangerous.

Hank stepped outside his room and followed the sounds. He heard distinct voices and words, angry men yelling at someone.

"Get down, on your stomach!"

"Listen or I'll shoot you!"

"I said, get down!"

"Stop struggling! Stop Struggling!"

Hank hurried up the hall and rounded the corner. He stopped when he saw the four men just outside one of the dorms. They had an old man pinned to the ground. Hank wasn't sure, but he thought …

"Imeko," he whispered.

One of the men put a knee in the small of Imeko's back. He had Imeko's hands pulled behind his back and ran a pair of zip ties around his wrist. He cinched them tight, binding Imeko's wrists together. From where Hank stood, he saw blood spilling from one of Imeko's palms. Two men lifted him up by his arms, and Imeko let out a cry of pain.

"Hey!" Hank yelled and hurried to where the five men were, trying his best not to run and appear intimidating or angry. He only wanted to look concerned. "Hey. What's going on?"

One of the men looked up at him. He was younger than Hank, his eyes dark, as well as his hair. A full beard covered the lower part of his face, and he held a pistol in his hand.

"Stay out of this, sir," he said. He sounded like an angry cop with a power trip attitude.

Hank stopped about twenty feet from the scuffle. "What did he do?"

"Mind your business," Beard growled.

"He's an old man," Hank argued. "There's no need to manhandle him like that."

Imeko stopped struggling when he saw Hank. Blood dribbled from a wound on the side of his neck. They stared at each other, but the look in his eyes bordered on hate. "You," he said, his voice gruff and full of anger. "You are the death of us."

"What?"

"Walking man. You … you are one with the dead. You …"

"Shut-up," Beard said and jerked his arm, leading him away from the dorm room and Hank.

Hank watched as the four men led a no longer struggling Imeko away. The old guy looked back at Hank once and shook his head before facing forward and going with the men willingly. He wanted to follow them. He wanted to ask Imeko what he meant, but he didn't think it was a good idea. Beard and his buddies might not like it and might just decide to escort Hank to wherever they were taking Imeko, complete with his wrists zip tied behind his back, probably so tight his hands would go numb. Blood dripped on the floor behind them.

And what if they didn't? What if they let Imeko tell Hank what he meant? Is it something he really wanted to know? Is it something he wanted the four guards surrounding Imeko to know?

Not really.

Hank made his way to the bathroom where he relieved himself, and then went to the sink to wash his hands the best he could. The mirror was still shattered, but the shattered glass was nowhere to be seen, not in the sink or on the counter, or even on the floor anywhere. The mirror itself had strips of black tape on it, holding the remaining glass in place. What he could see of his image was nothing more than a jagged reflection who could have been someone else.

Imeko's words hung in his mind. He spoke them into the broken mirror.

"Walking man. You … you are one with the dead." He repeated it several times, then shortened it. "One with the dead. What did you mean by that, Imeko?"

Hank turned on the water and picked up the soap with his left hand. He rolled it over a couple of times and set it back on the basin, where it slid into its previous spot in a small puddle of scum. The water had grown warm by the time he rinsed his hand. He let the water run over it, his eyes focused on the soap scum, and his memory drifted back to when he was a kid.

It wasn't a sink he thought of but the shower. There had been a soap dish built into the wall. A white bar of Dove soap had always sat on it, and when wet, bubbles would spill off the dish and down the blue tiled shower wall. Over time the tiles were streaked, and the blue had faded where the soap scum had trailed.

Tears fell down his face as his memories shifted from the soap dish and scum of his childhood home to the bottles of liquid soap Jeanette liked to use.

"I like my bar soap," he had said on numerous occasions when she brought home liquid soap for men.

"Just try it, Hank."

His answer had always been no, and now Jeanette was gone. He would give anything for a bottle of men's liquid soap instead of the bar on the sink's basin.

Hank grabbed the bar of soap and threw it across the bathroom. It struck the wall with a loud thump, bounced off, and hit another wall before skidding across the floor. It came to a stop next to the toilet.

That's not wise, Hank.

48

"What was that?" he asked.

It's called a temper tantrum. The voice wasn't his, but Jeanette's.

"I know, but—"

Have you thought much about your bite marks?

"What does that have to do with anything?"

I think it has everything to do with what is wrong with you.

"There's nothing wrong with me."

"I didn't say there was."

Hank turned around to see a younger man, maybe in his mid-twenties, staring back at him. His eyes held suspicion in them. His brows were upside down Vs, and his forehead held the leery look of someone who is either confused or worried … or a little bit of both.

Heat filled Hank's face and trailed down his neck. He nodded to the guy and muttered a *hello* and *excuse me*, before walking out the bathroom. He ran a hand through his hair as he walked down the hall in the direction they took Imeko. He rounded the corner and stopped. Coming toward him was Harrison Avis. The air filled with a heavy aroma and grew thicker as Avis drew nearer. It was thick like cigar smoke. Hank sniffled as if his

49

sinuses were bothering him, taking in Avis's stench.

"Mr. Walker," he said and stopped a few feet from Hank.

"Mr. Avis," Hank responded.

"One of the guards said you got involved with them earlier."

One of Hank's brows lifted. "One of the guards said that?"

"Yes. What do you have to say about that?"

He had a feeling he knew what Avis was talking about, but he wasn't going to give in to him, especially since he's never been on the outside. "I haven't talked to any guards today. That's what I have to say about that."

"That's not what I was told."

"Then you were told wrong."

"Mr. Walker, we don't have to be like this."

Hank wanted to smile at this. He wanted to laugh out loud, maybe slap his knee for emphasis. He didn't do that.

"I agree. I don't want it like this, but you seem to not care much for me as it is, so if this is on anyone, it's you."

"You walked out of my office without answering any questions."

"I don't plan on answering any, either."

Hank went to walk by, but Avis grabbed his arm.

"You need to answer one question, Mr. Walker." There was an edge to his voice which told him Avis was serious, and he meant to get an answer, one way or another. He didn't care much for the tone. It was something he had heard before from people, like his former boss and bullies in school, and even one of the players on the rival baseball team in legion ball. The player was Mark Laughlin, the third baseman for Legion Seventeen. Laughlin had taken a brushback pitch from Robert Carrington of Legion Three, and he promptly hit the ground when he ducked away. There was a stare down and Laughlin pointed at Carrington and yelled something about shoving a bat where the sun don't shine. Carrington, like the hothead he was, dared him to try.

And it was game on. Laughlin ran at Carrington, who dropped his glove and started for him. Hank barely made it to the two guys before the first punch was landed (this would be Carrington

51

getting a right hook in as Laughlin charged him). The punch, though hitting home, did little damage as Laughlin tackled Carrington and they both went to the ground, halfway between home plate and the pitcher's mound. This is where Hank and Davey Blaylock and Louis Williams and the rest of Legion Three met the rest of Legion Seventeen.

It was Hank who pulled Laughlin from Carrington and pinned him to the ground. Through the fracas, Hank heard the anger in Laughlin's voice as he told him to "Get off me. Get off me."

The intent in his voice, though filled with the rush of adrenalin and anger, still didn't hold the same tone as Harrison Avis's did right then. Hank had come away with a busted lip on that occasion. He had a feeling things could be worse this go around.

Hank pulled his arm free from Avis's grip. "What's that?"

"What did that Indian mean with what he said to you earlier?"

Hank did smile this time. "So those are the guards you're talking about? The guys that roughed up an old man?"

"There's something wrong with that old man."

Hank nodded. "Yeah, I guess there is. It's not every day you see your family ripped apart and you lose everything and everyone you love. But I guess you don't know much about that, do you?"

Avis stuck a finger in Hank's chest, poking it with each word he spoke. "You watch your mouth, boy."

Hank didn't back up, and he didn't back down. He grabbed Avis's wrists and squeezed. It wasn't something he thought he would ever do, at least not in the living world. But this wasn't the living world. It was a dead one with few survivors left, and as far as Hank was concerned, a survivor was someone who actually had to deal with biters, who actually lost someone (or everyone, like Imeko), someone who felt fear, someone who felt pain, someone who put a bullet in a friend or family member's head after they died and turned. Avis was not a survivor.

"How did you get to be the leader of this place?" Hank asked. "How did you, someone who has never been out there, end up being in charge around here? Tell me how that happened."

53

"I can have you put out of here, Mr. Walker. Is that what you want?" Avis had the upper hand, and he knew it. He would play this hand out, and in the end, he would get his way.

"Maybe so," Hank said. He wasn't entirely sure Avis would do it, but he thought there was a better chance he would than he wouldn't. Hank needed to be careful. If he got kicked out, what were the chances Bobby or Jake or Hetch might try to fight for him? What were the chances they all got kicked out? The thought of his son being back out in the world where his mother died terrified him. With that, Hank's shoulders slumped, and his voice softened. He didn't feel as defeated as he sounded, but he was almost certain Harrison Avis believed he had won the battle, and maybe even the war. "What do you want to know?"

Avis smirked. "I told you already. I want to know what the Indian meant by what he said to you earlier."

"Which part?"

Hank knew good and well which part, but he didn't know Avis's intentions or what he had heard. He had a good feeling who he heard it from:

the bearded 'guard' who yelled at Imeko and told Hank to mind his business.

"He said you are death, you are one of the dead. What did he mean by that?"

Hank shook his head and gave the most honest answer he could, "I have no clue. I was wondering the same thing."

"So, you're trying to tell me you don't know a thing about what he said or why he said it?"

"I've had three encounters with him, Mr. Avis. The first time was when I saved him and a couple members of his family from a horde of biters. The second time was when I arrived here, and then maybe less than an hour ago. That's it. I don't know him. We're not friends. After I saved him and got his granddaughter where she needed to be, he made me leave. Your guess is as good as mine. If that's not good enough for you, I don't know what is."

"Should I ask him?"

"Feel free. I'd like to know the answer myself. Now, if you don't mind, I'm going to get something to eat. Okay?"

Avis said nothing. After several tense seconds Hank nodded. "Have a good day," he said and walked off.

As he went, he could feel Avis's angered stare boring a hole in the back of his head. He could feel the hate brewing up inside himself—hate for a man he knew even less than he did Imeko. He focused on the corner of the hall and when he rounded it, he felt relief sweep over him.

Hank went to the cafeteria and got a bowl of potato soup and freshly made bread that was slightly stiff, but not stale. The woman at the counter gave him a "hello," and a "have a nice day." He responded pretty much in kind while trying not to sniff the air for the pleasant scent coming from her.

He ate in silence and made his way back to his room. He lay on the bed and stared at the ceiling, much the same way he had when he was an angsty teenager (in much the same manner he guessed most teenagers of the old world once did).

His stomach grumbled and knotted. He swallowed down rising bile. A few minutes later his stomach settled, but not without a wave of exhaustion replacing the knots. Hank drifted toward sleep but woke to the raps on the door.

Hank sat up slowly. When the knock came again, it was accompanied by a voice. "Hank, you in there?"

He swung his legs off the bed and stood. His head swooned for a second and his hands went out to his sides in hopes of balancing out the world around him.

"Hank?" It was Jake and the longer he stood outside the door, the more anxious he sounded.

"Come in, Jake," he answered finally.

The door opened with a click and a squeal, and Jake stepped inside. He was still good old Jake, the youngest—and last surviving of Hank's brothers. His hair was short, and his jeans were loose but not baggy. Eddie from Iron Maiden was on his shirt, and he looked like he was in the cockpit of an airplane. Stubble lined his chin, and a chain ran from one belt loop to the wallet in his back pocket (not that he needed either of those things anymore. Habit is as habit does). He was tall and lanky and wore glasses that made him look smart (and he was).

"You okay?" Jake asked. There was a touch of worry in his eyes.

"Yeah. I fell asleep."

"You seem to be doing a lot of that since you got here."

"I guess almost dying does that to you."

"Maybe so."

Hank took a good look at his brother. Something was up, and he had forgotten the telltale sign until right then. Jake's neck twitched. It wasn't much, but Hank saw it and knew Jake had something on his mind.

"Everything okay, Jake?"

He shrugged and leaned against the wall, crossing his arms. He frowned and didn't look directly at Hank.

"What is it, little bro?"

Jake looked up. "They just put someone out."

Hank cocked his head to the side. "What do you mean they put someone out? Out of where?"

"Out of here. Out of this safe zone."

"Why would they do that? Don't they know putting people out could get them killed? No, scratch that, whoever they put out probably will get killed."

"I don't know why they are doing it. They just said he was dangerous to the camp and ..."

"Wait, Jake. How do you know that?"

"They had a meeting."

"What do you mean a meeting?"

"Didn't you hear the bell sound earlier?"

Hank shook his head. "No. I was asleep."

Jake pushed from the wall and paced the room. He raised his hand as if about to give a speech or lecture. "You must have been seriously asleep."

"I guess so." Hank stretched and let out a deep yawn. "Do you know the person they put out?"

"No. Well, not really, but you do."

Hank's brows lifted. "I do?"

"That Native American guy."

"Imeko?"

"Is that his name?"

"Short guy, gray hair, eyes that look black? Just a few doors down from here?"

"Yeah, that would be the one."

"Avis," Hank said and brushed by Jake out of the room. He was halfway up the hall before his brother caught up with him.

"Where are you going, Hank?"

"To have a little talk with that prick, Avis."

Jake stopped in the middle of the hall. Hank looked back at him when he reached the elbow leading to another part of the floor. "What?"

"Hank, Avis isn't one you want to mess with."

"Why do you say that?"

"There's something about him that scares me."

Hank nodded. "I think that's what he banks on—people being scared of him."

"Probably so."

"Jake, I'm not scared of him."

"Maybe you should be."

Hank Walker stood in the hallway, his baby brother less than twenty feet from him. The wide-eyed look on Jake's face told him Avis was a bad person, and Jake had probably seen more than he would ever admit. Still, he asked.

"Imeko isn't the first person Avis has put out since you've been here, is he?"

Jake shook his head.

"How many more?"

"At least four."

"He's put out five people since you've been here?"

"At least."

Hank looked down at the floor, the tile a speckled white and black with faded paths worn where people had walked. They were very much like the ruts in a dirt road or a footpath in the middle of the woods. But Hank really didn't notice the worn floor. He didn't really see anything. He was thinking of Avis and how angry the guy was because Hank argued with him. Hank didn't know him well, but he didn't like him. He knew this guy was bad news, and he thrived on intimidation. At this point, though, Hank had faced death, and death had almost claimed him. Why should he be afraid of Harrison Avis more than any other crazy person he had come across since all this began? Why should he be more afraid of him than the biters?

I'm not, he thought.

"Maybe he should be afraid of me."

"Hank."

"Stay here, little brother. I need some answers, and I don't want this creep to think you are with me on it.

"But I am with you, Hank," Jake responded.

"Then act like you're not, okay?"

Hank walked away, anger in his heart, heat on his face, and pain in his temples.

It's interesting how the mind works and memory kicks in, even over a short amount of time. Hank found the office with ease, went inside and passed the desks that used to belong to school secretaries.

"Excuse me, sir," one said. It was the pretty girl from earlier. She stood and tried to get his attention.

"Is Avis in there?" he asked and thumbed toward the principal's office, which was now nothing more than a place for a dictator to hold shop.

"Sir, I need you to—"

"That's what I thought." Hank opened the door.

Harrison Avis sat in the chair behind the desk. He looked up from a book, saw it was Hank, and slid a bookmark between the pages as he folded the book shut. On the desk was also a glass of water and a folder, a pen sitting on top.

"Have you finally come to talk with me, Mr. Walker?"

It certainly wasn't the question Hank expected. It also wasn't the question he really wanted to answer.

The door slammed behind Hank, helped along by a not so gentle shove. "Are you sending Imeko back out there?" Hank pointed toward the door. He had no idea if it was the direction of the front gates or not, but it was the direction Avis had pointed in their only other conversation in the room.

"You mean the Indian?"

"Native American. And yes."

"No, I'm not sending him back out there."

"That's not what I heard."

"I've already sent him out."

Hank stopped. They stared at each other in silence for thirty or so seconds. Avis flinched first. He glanced down at the book on his desk and then back up at Hank.

"Is there a problem?"

"You're a weak-minded dictator ..." Hank finally said.

"Watch yourself, Mr. Walker."

Hank placed both hands on Avis's desk. "You just sent an old man to his death."

"He'll be fine."

"How can you say that?"

"He survived before we brought him here. He'll survive now that he is back out there."

Hank's face grew hot. He clenched his teeth and his breaths were quick and shallow. The stench of Avis's cigar blood grew thick.

"Everyone here survived out there until they were brought here," Hank said through his teeth. "Everyone except for you."

"Mr. Walker, I'm not going to tell you again to watch yourself."

Hank swept his hand across Avis's desk. The book, folders (and the papers in them), the pen, and the glass of water slid from the desk. The glass shattered on the floor and the water splashed on the carpet and the side of the desk. Hank leaned over the desk, his face less than a foot from Avis's. He could smell the stench coming off him, from within him. Hank's stomach grumbled.

"Don't tell me to watch myself, you coward."

Avis stood, the chair rolling back behind him. He extended a hand, finger out, in Hank's direction.

"I warned you to—"

64

"Shut your trap, Avis," Hank said. His hand shot out, grabbing Avis's wrist. He turned his wrist, bending his arm down. Avis went with it. A grimace stretched across his face, and he let out what Hank thought was a startled yelp, and not one from the sudden pain he may have felt race up his arm and into his shoulder. "Who said you could put him out?"

Avis growled his answer out. "The committee did."

"What committee?"

"The committee who runs this place."

"Who is on this committee?"

"I can't give you that information."

Hank twisted Avis's wrist further. Avis leaned forward, his chest almost touching his desk.

"You're a liar," Hank said and released Avis's wrist.

Avis stood straight and rubbed his arm. He flexed his hand and glared at Hank. "You're going to regret that."

"I wouldn't threaten me, Avis. You're not going to get away with this. Putting an old man out there. You better hope he doesn't die."

"And what if he does?"

"You better hope he doesn't."

Hank turned away from Avis and grabbed the knob. He flung the door open. The knob hit the wall and bounced back after Hank was out. He passed the woman at the desk. Her eyes were wide and her mouth slightly ajar. The scent that rose off her was sweet and intoxicating. Hank's mouth grew wet and he licked his lips.

"Have a good day," he said and stopped. He turned around and looked at the woman. She was young and pretty and her eyes held fear in them. "What's your name?" he asked.

"Wha … what?"

"Your name. What's your name?"

"Wendy. Why?"

Her scent changed from sweet and intoxicating to what Hank could only think of as sour milk and copper. It was so sudden it was like someone sprayed the room with a particularly cloying air freshener that was no air freshener at all.

"Wendy, I'm not the bad guy here. The man in there is. He put out an old man. He put him out there, beyond those walls, where the biters roam, and they are hungry. They are always hungry. That old man doesn't stand a chance out there. Just keep that in mind when I ask you one question. Okay?"

She nodded.

"Who is on the committee that governs this place?"

Wendy frowned, shook her head slightly. She opened her mouth to speak, but nothing came out. She looked confused.

Hank looked to the principal's office, a place so many kids had probably feared over the years, probably right up until the dead claimed the world as their own. Avis stood in the doorway, still rubbing his wrist. Hank wished he had twisted it harder, at least hard enough to break.

"That's what I thought."

Hank left the office and made his way to the cafeteria. There he found Hetch and Jake. Bobby sat with the little girl he had been playing basketball with in the gym.

"Hi, Bobby," he said, but didn't sit at the table with them. The aroma spilling from them was soft and not quite as intoxicating as Wendy's had been. Hers made his mouth water, almost in a lustful manner. Theirs was different … innocent. "You doing okay?"

"Yeah, Dad. I'm okay."

"Good." He wanted to sit down, to hug his son, the last remaining piece of Jeanette he had. He wanted to grab him and never let him go. It would embarrass Bobby, but what if it did? Hank was his father and that's what fathers did to their kids. Instead, he smiled at the young lady and said to Bobby, "I'm going to be over there with Hetch and Jake, okay?"

"Okay." Bobby looked relieved, as if he knew what Hank had been thinking.

Hank sat at the table with Hetch and Jake. When he did, he knew something was wrong with his sense of smell. It had plagued him off and on since he woke up from his time near death, but over the last few hours it had intensified, grown more acute. He wasn't entirely sure, even though he might have thought it before, but what he believed he smelled right then (and had been every time someone was near him) was blood. Right then the blood he smelled was rich and lively, like a bold red wine.

"Did you go see Avis?" Jake asked, pulling him from his thoughts. He stuffed what looked like ravioli in his mouth and chewed.

68

"Yeah, I did."

"How'd that go?" Hetch asked.

"Not good."

"Really?"

"Really, Hetch."

"What happened?" Jake asked, and wiped his mouth with the back of one hand.

"I tried to break his arm."

Hetch almost spit out the water he was drinking. He caught himself, coughed into his hand several times. His eyes watered. He wiped at them. "You what?"

"Yeah. It got a little heated when he told me he has already put Imeko out."

"They've already put him out?" Jake asked. His fork was on his plate, both hands to either side of it.

"He," Hank stressed. "Avis already put him out."

"I thought the committee had to decide on that."

"There is no committee. It's just him."

"How do you know this?" Hetch asked.

Hank glanced at Bobby and the young lady. They were talking like young lovers would. He could see the gleam in their eyes. He knew the way they smiled at each other, the way she laughed at whatever he said. He knew puppy love when he saw it, but part of him thought maybe, in this world where love and friends and people who weren't crazy were so few, what he saw was the real thing and not the normal young infatuations. He turned back to Hetch and Jake.

"I asked Avis who was on the committee who voted Imeko out. He wouldn't tell me. When I left his office, I asked one of the women playing secretary the same question. She looked at me like she had no clue what I was talking about. If your secretary doesn't know the answer to a question like that, then someone is lying."

"Maybe she wasn't expecting the question," Jake said, took a swallow of water and picked his fork back up. A couple seconds later, another piece of ravioli went into his mouth. Ever the optimist. Hank was sometimes jealous of him. This moment was not one of those times.

"No, I don't think so. If I would have caught her off guard, then she still would have said something. Anything. It's what people do when they know the answer to a question they don't expect. They lie. She didn't lie. She didn't even attempt to. And why is that? Because she didn't know of any committee."

"How can you be so sure?" Jake asked.

"Gut instinct, maybe?"

"What if your gut is wrong?"

"I don't think it is. Really, it doesn't matter now anyway."

"Why is that?"

"I've pissed off the head honcho. I'm sure there is retaliation coming."

"You think he will boot you out?" Hetch asked.

"I do."

"We'll go with you," Jake said. His fork hung by his fingertips above the tray he had been eating from.

"No."

"Yes." Jake pointed the fork at his older brother. "We're family, Hank. We're all we have left."

Hank looked back to Bobby. He was smiling. The girl was smiling. Both had one hand on the table, holding the others.

"We might be family, but I'm not letting them put Bobby out of this place. I'll go willingly before I allow that."

Jake and Hetch both looked at Bobby and the girl.

"Are they holding hands?" Jake asked, his voice rising in pitch a little.

"That's what it looks like," Hetch said. A thin smile formed on his face.

"Well, they just need to stop with that mess," Jake said and started to stand.

"Sit down," Hank said. He pointed back at Jake's seat. "Now."

"But …"

"Don't have me embarrass you, little brother."

Jake looked around and then sat.

"No one is going anywhere if I can help it."

"What if they kick you out?" Jake asked.

Hank shrugged. "Answer me something."

"What's that?" Jake pushed his tray to his right. His elbows went on the table, his hands in front of his face, the fingers laced together as if he were about to lift up a prayer.

"How did y'all find out Avis was putting Imeko out?"

"The bell was rung," Hetch said. "Then we went out to the football field on the back side of the school. There is a wooden platform out there."

"It's kind of creepy," Jake interjected.

"How's that?"

"It kind of looks like a gallows from back in the old west days."

"Is there a crossbeam?"

"Yup," Hetch replied.

"Any nooses?"

"Nope, but I wouldn't doubt one could hang from there easily enough."

Hank nodded. "Okay, so everyone went out to this … this platform, right?"

"Then what?"

"Avis stood at the top of it," Hetch said. "Imeko stood beside him. His hands were bound behind his back like a prisoner. There were two guards on the platform with them."

"What for?"

"I don't know. Maybe they were there just in case Imeko tried anything."

"Did they have guns."

"Yes," Hetch said.

"Both of them," Jake added.

"They held guns on a harmless old man."

"They didn't seem to think he was harmless."

"They?"

73

"Avis and the two guards."

"Maybe he wasn't—he was holding his own against the dead the first time I met him. What else happened."

"They held court," Jake said. The glass of water was half empty now and he swished the liquid around in the glass.

"They put him on trial?"

"If that's what you want to call it."

"What would you call it?"

"They condemned him. He never got to talk."

"Did he try?"

Jake shook his head. "No. He didn't speak at all. He only stared out at the crowd."

"Yeah. His eyes were distant, kind of like he saw something no one else could."

Hank shook his head. "He's dead."

"Why do you say that?" Jake asked.

"He wanted to die. Remember Hetch? They picked him up, and he was sitting in the snow. He wanted to die, but you guys saved him."

"It was the right thing to do," Hetch protested.

"Maybe so, for someone else, but maybe not for him." Hank waved the subject off, dismissing it before Hetch could say anything else. "So, he was put on trial. Was any reason given to why Avis wanted him put out?"

"He said Imeko was dangerous, like a feral animal," Jake said.

"He said that?"

"He did," Hetch answered.

Hank glanced at Bobby. He and the girl were no longer talking. They sat across from each other, their hands still locked together, their eyes staring into each other's. A radiant glow surrounded them. It was as if the sun were shining down on them, casting its brilliant rays on the two young kids, approving of this blossoming romance. He looked back to his brother and friend.

"Did he put it to a vote?"

"No," they said in unison.

"He told them Imeko was dangerous, and they couldn't risk having him there," Hetch said.

"Avis called him a crazy Indian."

Heat rose in Hank's face again. He felt the blood pulse through his temples. The muscles in his jaw flexed, released, flexed again.

"Not only has he never dealt with the biters, he's a racist. That's just what this place needs."

"What?" Hetch asked. "What do you mean he's never dealt with the dead?"

"What did I say? He's never dealt with a biter. Never had to kill one. Never seen anyone ripped apart."

Images flooded Hank's memories: Pop being bitten and his back clawed through by bony fingers; Lee bitten by a Paul Marcum look-alike; Davey Blaylock leading a swarm of the dead away from Hank after one sank its teeth into him; Fat Boy squirming on the side of Old Batesburg Road after Hank shot him several times and then let a female biter loose on him; The Chosen Ones, they just couldn't let the one parishioner go, and he was the one who got them in the end … along with the horde that had trundled along after Hank; the little girl …

He shook his head, forcing back the memories the best he could.

"How do you know this?" Jake asked.

"It's pretty much what he said a couple of days ago, the first time I met him. He was trying to interrogate me under the guise we would have a friendly chat. There was nothing friendly about it. I don't think either of us liked each other from the get-go. None of this really matters," Hank continued. "You guys said a bell was rung, right?"

"Yup," Hetch replied.

"Where is it?"

"I think it is near the back of the school, not too far from the football field."

"We need to ring it."

"What?" Jake asked. His eyes were slightly wide. Hank could see the gray in them. But there was something else—fear.

"Don't worry, little brother," he said. "I'll take care of everything else if one of you can ring the bell."

"I'll do it," Jake said. There was no hesitancy in his voice at all.

"No," Hetch said. "I'll do it—I don't have anyone here, so if I get caught, at least no one else will get thrown out with me."

"Are you sure?" Hank asked.

"Yeah."

Hank nodded and stood.

"What are you going to do, Hank?" Jake asked.

Hank took a deep breath. "Expose a fraud. And try not to get myself killed."

"When do you want to do this?" Hetch inquired.

"Tonight."

"Tonight?"

"Yeah, after most everyone has gone to bed. We wake them up with the bell ringing. I'll be on the platform waiting."

Hank knew it was risky. He also knew if he did nothing, he would be gone by the morning anyway. He had questioned the authority of South Carolina Fort Survivor Number Three's leader (by default, he guessed). And it might not only be him. It could cost Bobby and Jake the safety of the compound as well.

He walked away. As he did so, he patted Bobby on the shoulder, but said nothing. He wasn't sure he could right then without tearing up or fear of what could happen on his face, so maybe it was better he didn't.

He left the cafeteria and made his way to his room along a path that had become familiar in the few days since he woke up. He stopped a few doors down from his room, at the door standing open to the room Imeko had occupied as recently as that morning, then stepped inside.

The blankets and bed sheets were crumpled and clinging to the edge of the bed. The pillows were shoved against the headboard. There were clothes on the floor, the small dresser off to the right of the door had been toppled over, and a mirror opposite the bed had been broken. There was blood on the floor near it. Hank thought back to earlier when he saw Imeko struggling with the guards. There had been blood on one palm and his neck. Now Hank wondered if Imeko didn't try to kill himself.

Or maybe he tried to kill one of them.

He walked toward the broken mirror and stopped just short of the dresser. Laying between the wall and the dresser was Humphrey. Hank picked her up.

"Hi, old friend," he said. Even though there was no glass or dirt on her, he brushed her off as if there were. "How have you been?"

He didn't expect an answer and didn't get one.

"Well, it was good to see you again," he said and walked over to the bed. He set Humphrey where the pillow should have been. "See you around."

Hank shoved one hand in his pocket. The other one had bandaged knuckles, so he hung his thumb in the pocket and let his hand dangle. He left the room but turned back to catch a glimpse of

Humphrey one last time. The bear was just that, a stuffed bear in bunny pajamas. There was no terrified little girl inside to beg him to stay.

At his room, he closed the door but didn't lock it. He thought about it. In the end, his thoughts were simple. *If they want me, they'll get me with or without the door locked.*

He went to the bed and reached beneath the pillow. The notebook was there. He picked it up and flipped through it, scanning the pages but not really reading any of it. When he reached the end of the writing, there were still several blank pages left. He flipped one more page, separating what he wrote before to what he was about to write. He reached into the end table and pulled out an old ball point pen. He tested it on the backside of the previous page, making a black circle looping itself several times.

He didn't bother dating the page. He wasn't too sure he knew the actual date anyway. At the top he simply wrote *If I Leave.*

To Bobby, he wrote in his not-so-neat script. He paused, not sure what to say. His mind kept going back to his son and the girl, the way they stared at each other. If Hank had to leave, at least Bobby would have someone here who could comfort him. And he would have Jake, too. Jake could take care of him. He put the pen to paper and wrote.

If you are reading this, then I am gone, either by my own will or because I was put out. Either way, I want you to know I love you and always will. Jake will be here for you, to raise you the best he knows how. Don't give him too much of a hard time, okay?

You're a strong kid. You take after your mother, and I am thankful for that. Keep your heart of gold and never change, even in this world that has changed so much and so many people for the worse.

Harrison Avis is a bad man. He is dangerous. He should not be in power here. Though I am gone, it is not without a purpose. It's to protect you and the people here from people like Avis ... and like me. I can't stay here, Bobby. There is something wrong with me. I just recently figured this out. Imeko said I was dead, that I would be the end of this place if I stay. I believe he is right. For that reason alone, I have to leave, but not before I make things right for this place.

Know I will always love you. Always.

Love,

Dad

Hank read the note and cringed. It was all over the place. He wasn't sure how to tell Bobby he could smell the blood of every person he encountered. He wasn't even sure he understood it himself, but he knew the scent of blood was as intoxicating as alcohol to a drunk, crack to a druggie, and smokes to a nicotine addict. He also knew it was the bite. He may not have died and turned into one of those things outside the wall, but the wound had done something to him. What that something was he didn't know, but he had a feeling he wouldn't be able to control himself when the craving hit. That's what it was, after all—a craving. One begging for something he didn't want to think about.

A knock came at the door. Hank looked up from the notepad and waited for another knock. His heart raced, and he licked his lips. He focused on the doorknob, expecting it to turn at any second and a group of Avis's henchmen to pour into the room, guns drawn. They might even shoot him where he sat. Hank closed the notepad without thinking about it. He set it on the bed, the pen on top.

Another knock came, this one followed by a voice, but not the one he expected. "Hank, open up."

He stood and exhaled in relief. He opened the door. Hetch stood in the hall. He wore blue jeans and a dark shirt. He glanced over his shoulder, as if looking for someone who may have followed him.

"Come on in." Hank closed the door behind Hetch. "What's up?"

"It's late, Hank. If we're going to do this, we should probably go ahead and get it over with."

"Are you sure you want to do this?"

"Are you?"

"Yes," Hank said. "Before we do this, can I ask you a question?"

"Sure, man. What is it?"

"Have you … have you had any … I don't know … side effects from being bitten?"

"What?"

Hank shrugged. For the first time since being bitten at the lake, he wasn't sure what to say or even how to say it. He recalled standing in the shower, the water cold and not more than a trickle by the time he was done. There had been so much blood—blood that belonged to the biters he had slain, as well as the blood of the little girl he accidentally shot and killed. The blood wasn't what told him he had been bitten. It was the sting of the soap in the wound. It was the candle on the toilet seat, its flame a steady unmoving light. Then bringing the flame to the wound, he knew he had been given the death penalty by good old Ma Nature. It was clear she had been pissed when she unleashed the virus which claimed billions of people around the world—and it was going to claim him, as well. But it didn't happen. It came close, but it didn't happen.

Hank lived and ended up here, thanks to Hetch and a bunch of former military guys.

"Have you had some interesting ... I don't know ... have you smelled anything interesting?"

Hetch's nose crinkled up and the left side of his upper lip lifted. "I don't understand what you are asking, buddy."

Hank ran a hand through his hair. He walked over to the window, lifted the blinds, and stared out into the darkness. There were no lights to be seen. It was an eerie sight—knowing there were guards on the walls and no lights to point them out, or at least to cast a shadow. He knew they were out there; they had guns, and if he wasn't careful he might get shot before he made it to the football field and the platform.

He turned back to Hetch, "How do you feel?"

"I feel fine. Why?"

"I don't."

"What do you mean? Are you sick?"

Hank shook his head. "Nothing like that. I … I'm just not sure. Something's wrong and I'm not sure what."

"Go to the infirmary and get checked out. There's a real sweet nurse there. Totally cool. Easy on the eyes, too."

"I don't think she can help me."

"If you're sick, she may have some medicine she can give you. I know they have a stockpile of all sorts of drugs—"

"That's the problem, Hetch. I don't think any drug can help me. I think … I think whatever is wrong with me is a direct symptom of being bit and almost dying."

"I was bit, Hank, and I'm fine."

"You never got close to dying."

Hetch nodded. "No, I never came close, but I sure thought I was going to."

"I was close," Hank said. He was looking out the window again. His eyes had adjusted enough so he could see the far wall on the south side of the one-time school turned survivor camp. "I was so close."

"Do you remember much about that? You know, about almost dying?"

"Yeah, I do." His breath fogged the window in front of him. It was the truth, he really did remember a lot. Being sick, the itching and burning of his skin, and the stomach cramps were a nightmare. His lungs felt thick and full of fluid. His head pounded. It was as if someone took a hammer to his skull over and over and over again. His hands and muscles cramped, and his vision dimmed as each hour passed. He meant to put himself down in the room where he thought Hetch would die. He had somehow made it there with Pop's shotgun. He had managed to get his socks off, but before he could do the deed, he lost consciousness.

That is where things changed, he guessed. He was dead. He knows this now just as he knew he was about to die then.

"I died," he said.

Hetch laughed. "We got to you in time, Hank."

"Maybe in time to revive my body, but I died, at least part of me did."

"Hank, that's crazy. You would have been a biter if you died."

Hank spun from the window. His eyes were wide and wild, his mouth was slightly open. "What did you say?"

Hetch put his hands out in front of him and took a step back. "Hey, I didn't mean anything by that, but—"

"No. No, I'm not mad. What did you say?"

"You would have been a biter if you died."

"That's it," Hank said. He wasn't looking at Hetch, but at the floor. His head shook from side to side as he walked around the room, a hand over his mouth, and his eyes wider than before.

"What? What is it?" Hetch grabbed Hank's shoulders and made him face him. "What is it?"

"Remember when you were bitten?"

"How can I forget?"

"Remember when we drove to Newberry after you had gotten better?"

"Yeah, what about it?"

"You went into that Wal-Mart and came out, and the biters acted like you weren't even there. Remember?"

"I remember quite well, Hank. What's the point?"

"The point is you are infected, but the water saved you. You didn't die, so you didn't become one of them. But they couldn't smell you, so they didn't try to eat you."

"Okay. What if that is the case?"

"It's like … I don't know … camouflage."

"Camouflage? Hank, I think you're reaching."

"Maybe so, but if the only side effect you have is that you don't get noticed by the dead, then that is awesome. I can't say that."

Hank went back to the window. He put a hand to it and felt the cold from outside on his fingertips. He pulled away, made a fist, released it, and turned back to Hetch.

"Listen, it will take me a few minutes to get to the football field from here. Give me a little time and then just start ringing the bell, okay?"

Hetch smiled. "Would you rather do this by flashlight?" He pulled two small lights—what they would have called Wal-Mart specials not more than a year earlier. One was red, the other was gray, and both fit neatly in the palm of your hand. There was a strap at the butt end of each one, the on-off button right beside it.

Hank returned the smile and reached for one.

"Red or gray?"

"Gray," Hank said. "I don't need anything drawing any extra attention to me."

"Are you sure about this?"

"I have to be. Whether or not Avis plans on putting me out the way he did Imeko, this community needs to know who he is." Hank walked to the door, then stopped. He turned to Hetch, who was right behind him. "He interviewed you, right?"

"Avis?"

"Yeah."

"He did."

"Did he tell you anything about himself?"

"No."

"I didn't think so." He opened the door. "Let's get this over with."

89

They went down the hall quietly, stopping only at Imeko's room. "Do me a favor," Hank said.

"What's that?"

"There is a teddy bear on Imeko's bed. When I'm gone, I need you to get that teddy bear—her name is Humphrey—and give it to Bobby. Tell him it is from me. Can you do that?"

"Yeah. No problem."

They said nothing else until they reached the exit doors leading out of the building. The cold air bit into Hank's exposed face and hands. There was still a bit of snow on the ground, something Hank still found difficult to believe considering they were in South Carolina, and snow like this hasn't fallen and stuck for years. But here it was, a couple of weeks after it fell and there was still some left on the ground. It amazed him.

"Thank you, Hetch," Hank said.

"You're welcome, my friend."

Hank nodded. He hated goodbyes and had said many over the last year. Most goodbyes were permanent. He hoped this one wouldn't be, but deep inside he believed it was.

"You ready?" Hetch asked.

"Wait for me to flash the light. I'll do it twice. As soon as I do, just start ringing the bell."

"Got it. And Hank?"

"Yeah?"

"Be careful."

"You, too."

Hetch went to the left and along the sidewalk hugging the building. Hank turned right and stayed on the sidewalk until he reached the fence leading to the backside of the school. He stopped short of the gate to the football field and the dirt track surrounding it.

You don't have to do this, Hank.

He wanted to believe it. More than anything, he wanted to believe he didn't have to try and expose Harrison Avis for the monster *(fraud)* he was. If he had thought longer and harder on it, he might have even convinced himself Avis only did what was best for the community, for the survivors. He didn't believe this theory at all, that Avis's decisions were all for the good of the people he was charged with protecting. No, Hank didn't believe Avis was capable of such a noble characteristic.

He let out a breath, one that seemed to deflate him all at once. "I have to do this."

It wasn't only that Hank thought Avis wasn't a good leader with noble intentions. He thought Avis was a bad *person*.

"And bad people don't need to be around my son."

There it was—the truth. It had nothing to do with the community, but more of a selfish, parental need to protect his kid. *That's not very noble, either*, he thought. Moreover, he knew if he were to ask the other survivors about outing a creep like Avis because he wanted nothing more than to keep him away from his kid, they would say he was worse than their fearless leader. He supposed he could let everything go, including Avis putting Imeko back out into the world of the dead, if only he had experienced the world the way most, if not all, the other survivors there had. And there was the rub in his head: the man, when questioned about his experience *out there* gave no real answer, either because he couldn't relive it (what Hank wanted to believe) or because he didn't live it at all (what Hank really believed).

"And he put others out there, as well," Hank whispered. His voice, though low, sounded like it echoed in the cold night.

You can still back out.

"No. I'm afraid I can't." The words came out on a plume of white vapor and swirled in front of him before dissipating into the night air.

There was no way around it. There might have been if he had cooperated fully with Avis from the beginning. Jeanette might have even told him to just do as he says so Bobby would be safe. And he would have listened, even if it had been only her voice in his head. But her voice never came, and he didn't cooperate, but called Avis out on it and then challenged him. No, there was no way around it at all.

Hank lifted the catch on the gate and pushed it open. He didn't bother pushing it closed and locking it back. In a few minutes people would pour through it anyway. Why give them one more obstacle on this cold late night?

The field had snow on it. Though it had thinned out and some had melted away when the temperature rose to above freezing a day or two ago, there was still plenty here. It was more like

93

slush now and in another few days it would be gone, maybe even by tomorrow afternoon if it warmed up a little. For now, it crunched under Hank's weight, sounding like shots from a gun. He tried to walk softly, but even that didn't keep the icy snow from crumbling beneath his boots.

The platform came into view. It sat near midfield, and it was just as Hetch and Jake had said—it looked like gallows. Hank swallowed what little saliva was on his tongue. For the briefest of seconds an image flashed in his mind. Harrison Avis stood on the platform, a broad smile on his face, an evil gleam in his eyes. He was looking down through a hole in the floor. To his right, a rope swayed back and forth. The rope was attached to the platform's crossbeam. Hanging from the other end was Hank, his neck broken, and his head tilted sideways. His tongue jutted from purple lips and blood spilled from his nose. His eyes were open and bulging.

Hank shook his head and fought back a sudden urge to turn and run, to get off the field and away from the platform, to get back through the gate and lock it back before he continued fleeing back to his room, where he would crawl into bed and pull the blankets all the way up to his non-bulging eyes.

Another deep breath and he made his way to the steps leading up to the platform. There were wooden handrails to either side of the steps he didn't use. His boots scuffed along each plank. When he reached the top, he had a dizzying moment of vertigo. He put his hands out to his sides to balance himself until it passed.

Hank walked to the center of the plank. He wanted to flick the flashlight on to see if there was a trapdoor beneath the crossbeams but stopped before he could press the button. Hetch might see it and ring the bell before Hank was ready.

It brought him to the reality before him—was he ready?

"No," was the short and accurate answer, and the one that tumbled from his lips just before he held the flashlight up and pressed the button before he lost his nerve. The light shined bright, but barely cut a swath in the darkness above his head. He pressed it three more times: Off. On. Off.

Then, like on Sunday mornings when he was a kid and the church bells would ring, signaling the beginning of either services or Sunday School, the hollow tone of a steel clapper smashing the inside of a large bell echoed through the night. It sent shivers along Hank's spine. The gong came again, the sound reverberating for several seconds, reminding Hank of an old horror movie he saw when he was a kid (one far too young to actually watch something so scary). The main character was a woman, and she was running through a church cemetery. The church bell began to ring, and it was the same hollow gong he heard. Then the dead began to rise from the graves, their hands tearing through the grass, fingers sinking into the ground and pulling their decaying bodies free from their final resting places. It wasn't too much different from what had happened to the world, only the dead didn't crawl from graves. They only stood from where they died and began killing the living.

The woman ran into the church where she thought it was safe, only to run into the man responsible for the demise of the other characters in the movie up to that point. She begged for help but realized a moment too late the good preacher with the black robe and shifty eyes wasn't going to do much helping at all. She screamed that bloody horror queen scream when she turned around to see walking corpses reaching for her. They looked nothing like the real dead just outside the walls of the fort and all over the world. They were only people in a black and white movie who may or may not have been wearing some sort of make up to give their skin a sunken look or a paler pallor. Still, it had been effective, whatever they had done, and it had scared young Henry Walker bad enough for him to scamper behind the couch, cup his hands over his ears, and clamp his eyes shut.

He heard the murmur of voices. Then the metal halide lights came on, and the field was washed in a bright glow. Hank shielded his eyes at first with one hand and watched as the sleepy people who lived at South Carolina Fort Survivor Number Three slowly poured onto the field through gates on either end. They reminded him of the dead in that horror movie, not rotting and not really moaning or groaning or even in a hurry to get at the flesh of the living.

The bell rang one last time. The same hollow sound seemed to echo for much longer, now that it had grown silent.

Hank heard Harrison Avis before he saw him.

"What are you doing?"

Hank turned. Avis stood at the top of the steps. His hands looked too large as he held onto the wooden rails. His hair was slightly ruffled, and he wore the same clothes from their last meeting. it was as if he hadn't been asleep for long, if at all.

At first Hank was startled. He hadn't expected Avis to appear on the platform. Shades of the image that scampered across his mind earlier came rushing back. He could almost see the smile on Avis's shadowed face. As quickly as before, the image was gone.

"I asked you a question. What are you doing?"

"Waiting on you," he said as calmly as he could.

"What's this all about?" someone yelled from below. A couple others chimed in as well, all wanting to know why they had been woken in the middle of a cold night by the bells.

"Listen," Hank said as loud as he could, trying to project his voice so he wouldn't have to yell. "You have a dangerous man in your presence. Someone who has never had to deal with the horrors beyond these walls. Someone who—"

"Seize him," Avis yelled.

A couple seconds later, three men appeared on the platform, each in military fatigues and carrying guns.

What did Hank expect would happen? He didn't really believe Avis would actually let him speak his peace, did he? He couldn't have believed it. It never happens that way, not in the old world, and certainly not in this new one.

"Wait!" Hank yelled.

One of the men stopped, while the other two continued forward. Hank got his hands up just in time to be struck with the butt of a rifle in the forearm. The pain was sharp, and his arm went limp immediately. The other guard grabbed Hank by the same arm and by the back of his neck.

What happened next was defensive instinct. With one arm twisted and the goon holding it shoving his head down, Hank reacted with an upper cut to his crotch. The man's knees buckled, and he released Hank's arm and neck as he collapsed to the floor, holding himself with both hands.

Hank went to stand but fell to his knees when the other guard punched him in the side of the head. His ear rang and his vision doubled for a few seconds. He shook his head and pitched forward when the second goon shoved him in the back with one foot. He heard the chambering of a bullet and realized it could all end any second.

There was the sound of a gun shot, but it wasn't near his head or body. It was one from off in the distance. The instant he heard the shot, he also heard where it hit—goon number two screamed and dropped his weapon. A spatter of blood struck Hank's face. He rolled over to see number two clutching his arm, blood spilling from between his fingers. There were tears in his eyes, and his lips were pulled back into a tortured grimace.

The third guard—the one who stopped when Hank yelled—now had his gun up. He spun, pointing his weapon here and there, but couldn't tell where the shot came from. Guard number two was no longer screaming, but he lay on the floor, holding his arm and whimpering as blood pooled beneath him. Avis had descended a couple steps. Both arms were over his head as if flesh and bone could stop a high caliber bullet.

"Where is he?" Avis yelled.

"I don't know," Number Three replied and spun around. His head swiveled on his neck, his eyes wide with fear.

Hank sat up and looked around. He didn't know who had shot Number Two, but he thought if he got out of this mess, he would like to shake the man's hand.

"Don't move," Number Three said and pointed the gun at Hank's head.

"Put the gun down," the voice came from out of the darkness. It was loud and full of intent, echoing in the night as if it came through a megaphone. "Put the gun down or the next bullet will be the one that ends your life."

It was all Hank could do to not smile. He didn't know where Jake had gotten the rifle from, but he knew he was a good shot—probably the best of all the Walker brothers, and he had nailed Number Two in a place that wouldn't kill him unless they didn't try and stop the blood flow.

Number Three held the gun on Hank a little longer. "Where is the shooter?" he asked.

"Your guess is as good as mine," he answered. "But I think he means business."

"Put the gun down! I will not tell you again!"

"You might want to listen to him, buddy," Hank said.

Number Three looked around, his head nervously jerking about. Then he knelt and set the gun on the floor of the platform. He lifted his hands above his head.

"What are you doing?" Avis yelled from his crouched spot on the steps, his hands still covering his head the best they could.

Number Three looked at him with a wide-eyed stunned expression. "I'm not getting killed for you," he said.

Hank stood, not bothering to pick up the gun. "You know, don't you?" he whispered.

Number Three said nothing but gave a quick nod that was barely perceptible.

"It ends today," Hank said, then added, "get your friend some help or he'll bleed to death." Then he turned to face the crowd. Many had ducked down, and like Avis, they had their hands over their heads, cowering in fear.

"Please," Hank spoke. "Don't be afraid. No one is going to hurt you. Not anymore."

He didn't know if it was the right thing to say. He really didn't know if Avis had hurt anyone, other than those he put out, but his gut told him he had. His gut told him anyone who may have been a threat to Avis had been put out, or maybe even hung from the platform he stood on.

"Please," he repeated. "Stand up. There is no need to be worried for your safety, at least not from me."

Hank turned toward Avis, who was no longer crouched a few steps down from the landing. His hands no longer covered his head. He glared at Hank with all the malice of an angry bully who was just put in his place.

Not yet, Hank thought, *but shortly*.

"How many of you came here or were brought here seeking shelter from the dead world outside these walls?"

There was a murmur. Folks looked around at each other, then one by one at first, people raised their hands like they did when they were in grade school and knew the answer to a question the teacher posed. After the first few hands raised, more followed.

"Yeah, me too," Hank said. "We've all lost someone ... or *everyone* we know and love."

Though it wasn't a question, more hands went up, this time in rapid succession.

Hank looked back at Avis. He was on the top step now, his hands balled in tight fists. Number Three tended to Number Two. He had pulled his coat off and was wrapping his shirt around Number Two's forearm. Number One, who had been crotch-punched at the beginning of the struggle was now sitting up, his hands still between his legs. His eyes were puffy, as if he had been crying. Beside him was a puddle of vomit Hank didn't recall seeing him release.

"How many of you had to go through an interview after you arrived here?"

More hands went up. It appeared as if everyone in the crowd had a hand in the air. Hank turned and looked at the guards. "What about you guys? Did you get interviewed when you arrived?"

Number One and Number Three nodded. Number Two said nothing and made no affirmative motion, but Hank didn't think he would. He lay on his back, the shirt wrapped around his arm. Hank could see blood through the cloth.

"Hey, you," he said and took a few steps toward the guards. "I want you to get him to the nurse. Take him now. Get that wound stitched up."

Number Three nodded. "Come on, Sean," he said and took Number Two's other arm.

Hank looked at Avis. "Let them by."

Avis's jaw flexed, but he stepped aside as the two guards passed him and made their way down the steps.

"Can someone help them to the infirmary, please? They were only doing what they were told to do."

Again, he looked back at Avis. It was almost like a dare. When he was a kid, Pop would give him a similar look, one that said, "I told you not to do something, now just you go ahead and do it and see what happens." He supposed that was what he was doing. A good old dare. *Go ahead, come on over here, Avis. Let's have a talk. One on one. Man to … whatever you are.*

Avis didn't take the dare. He looked like he wanted to, and Hank thought he would, but he would wait until the right moment, the moment Avis thought Hank wasn't watching him. It was okay, though. Hank knew, if anything, Jake was somewhere in the dark where Avis couldn't see him and if the leader of the compound tried anything, a bullet would zip his way. It would either be a warning shot or a life ending shot. Jake wouldn't miss his target.

Hank turned back to the crowd. "Who did your interviews?"

A chorus of voices rang out, saying either, Harrison Avis or Avis.

"Were you allowed to ask questions?"

Again, the voices rang out, all with varying degrees of "No."

Hank looked at Avis. He had taken a step or two forward. Hank didn't smile, but his hunch Avis would try to strike soon was beginning to play out.

"Harrison Avis has lost nothing. He has never faced the dead. He has never seen a person killed and then get up and try to kill him. Yet, he puts people out, people he deems dangerous."

Another glance back at Avis. He had taken another couple steps forward. Any minute now, he would either rush at Hank or he would go after one of the three guns laying on the platform's floor.

"People like a seventy-year-old man who lost his entire family before being brought here."

Another shot echoed in the night. It struck the platform to Hank's left. He turned to see Avis with his hands up, his eyes wide and his mouth slightly open. It was clear he had been reaching for one of the guns.

"This is a dangerous man," Hank said and pointed at him. "Have any of you lost a loved one thanks to this man?"

"I have," came the voice of a woman midway from the front. She had her hand in the air. Hank could see the wedding ring on her left hand.

Then several others came forward with "yes," or "I have" or "me, too."

"I think it's time for a new leader. One who will do things honestly."

"Yeah," many people cried out.

"I also think Mr. Avis should be sent beyond the walls, but not permanently. I believe he should go find the seventy-year-old man he banished yesterday. When he finds him, he can come back."

He turned to face Avis, whose hands were still in the air.

"If he is alive."

Turning back to the survivors, he asked one more question. "If you agree, say so."

And they said so.

The platform began to shake with the heavy footfalls of someone running. Hank turned to see Avis coming at him. He braced himself for a hit that came just a second later, but one he was able to anticipate with a solid punch to the back of Avis's head. They both fell to the hard wood floor of the platform, but it was Avis who was dazed and out of sorts.

Hank shoved Avis off him, knocking his head into the floor. He stood and looked down at Avis, who held his head in both his arms. Turning back to the assembled crowd, Hank pointed down at Avis.

"This is your leader—is this what you want? Someone who would attack another person when he isn't looking?"

More murmurs came from those who were sleeping fifteen minutes earlier and were now wide awake.

"It's time we removed the real dangerous person here."

The survivors agreed with a roar of shouts and a few cheers.

"You've heard the people, Avis," Hank said as he stared down on the man. "It's time you face what the rest of us have."

"You can't do this," Avis said. He sat up and was rubbing the back of his head. His breath came in hyperventilating gasps.

"Is that what all the people you put out said?" Avis didn't respond.

"Did they beg you to not put them out?"

When no answer came, Hank knew the answer.

"How many of them begged you not to put them out? How many of them cried? How many of their families or friends begged you not to send them out?" Hank was yelling now.

Avis stared hard at Hank, his bottom lip curled into a sneer, his eyes thin slits.

Hank's eyes narrowed. "You're not getting out of this. You can't."

"I can."

"I don't think so."

Hank turned back to the crowd, who were growing restless.

"I say we send him out now."

"What?" Avis yelled.

"We send him out tonight—right now—and if he can last a week out there, and if Imeko is still alive, we let him come back. All in favor, say 'aye.'"

What he heard was a song of "ayes."

"Let's go," Hank said and picked up one of the rifles. He pointed it at Avis. "Get up."

"You don't want to do this, Walker."

"You're right," Hank responded. "I don't want to do this, but you leave me little choice."

"How? We can work something out. You don't have to put me out."

"I have to, but at least you have the option to come back. You just have to survive for a week, which is probably a little longer than any of the people you put out lasted."

They left the platform, Avis in front, the weapon in Hank's hand pointing at the ground. He wanted to put it in Avis's back, to let him know he was there and any stupid move could be the last move he made. Hank also didn't want to appear like he was leading Avis to the gate at gunpoint, though that was exactly what was happening.

"Do we get food or a weapon?" Avis asked.

"Did you give food or a weapon to those you put out?"

Avis's mouth dropped open. This told the entire story of what he did.

"That's what I thought," Hank said and then added, "You're a real piece of work, Avis. You put people out, and you didn't give them food or a way to protect themselves, and now you want that very courtesy. I don't think so."

The moon made its way beneath the horizon. The sun would make its way up soon, but for now, there was an eerie darkness to the world. The gates opened on a track with wheels and the strength of three men pushing it. The sound of the wheels rattling on the track made Hank's skin swim with goose bumps. The dead had accumulated through the night and ran into the metal and wood stakes surrounding the fort, with the exception of the entrance. Those biters were shot from the high walls and dropped where they were.

"Let's go," Hank said. He hated the coldness in his voice. He hated knowing there was a good chance Avis would not last the day. He didn't want to put him out, but if not Avis, then before the day was out, it would have been Hank ... and maybe

111

Bobby, Jake, and Hetch, as well. It's not a chance he wanted to take.

"You're really going to do this?" Avis asked. His eyes were big, and his face was pale.

"Absolutely."

The two men stepped outside the gate. It had barely been half an hour since the survivors elected to send Harrison Avis outside the walls. Many were still up and hadn't gone back to bed. They all followed Hank and Avis to the front gate and watched as the gate opened. They watched as the two men stepped outside. Many of them flinched when the guards took shots at the handful of biters shambling near the gate. They all looked on in shock as Hank turned to face the men at the gate, who were waiting for him to step back in and leave Avis out in the world by himself.

"Close the gate," Hank said.

"What?" Jake blurted out. He didn't hold a rifle in his hand, and he had caught up to them at some point before they reached the gate.

"Jake, Hetch will explain everything. For now, I need to leave, just as Avis does. If we find Imeko alive, we'll be back."

"What if you don't?"

Hank shrugged, but his eyes never left Jake's. "Then one of us definitely won't be back."

"Hank—"

"Like I said, talk to Hetch. He'll explain everything the best he can. Okay?"

Jake shook his head and had been the entire brief time they talked. "You better come back, Hank."

Hank gave a non-committal nod. "I'll be seeing you around, little bro." To the men at the gate, "Close it."

Avis and Hank watched as the gate trundled along its track and clanged shut and listened to the sound of metal pipes sliding into place, locking the gate to all outsiders and biters alike.

"What are you going to do to me?" Avis asked, his voice shaky.

"Nothing," Hank answered and started away.

"Why did you come out with me?"

"I didn't."

Avis frowned. All around the dead who had run into the stakes moaned. Hank slid his knife from his back pocket, flicked it open, and drove the blade into the temple of the nearest biter, a woman with a mostly bald head and sunken eyes. Her lips

113

were missing, and she was not much more than skin on bones.

"Then what are you doing?" Avis asked. He looked disturbed by Hank putting down the biter. His eyes focused on her and not on Hank.

"I have one goal, Avis, and that is to find Imeko. For your sake, you better hope he's alive and not dead … or worse."

"Or worse?"

"That's what I said."

"What's worse than death?" Avis seemed to have gained a little more of his cockiness. The scared, high-pitched kid's voice he seemed to have adopted since Hetch rang the bell had faded back to his adult "I'm better than everyone" tone.

"You see these creatures who walk around eating others? They were once living, breathing people. Someone's mom or dad, sister or brother, wife or husband. They were someone's child at one time. That is far worse than death these days."

Avis said nothing. It seemed to be the way he did things these days. He lost his smug, "I am the boss" attitude. Along with it went his intimidation factor, something Hank thought was the hallmark of everything Harrison Avis did at the survivor

114

camp. He remembered the first meeting he had with Avis. Hank had thought he was military or maybe a shrink—he still thought he was probably a head doctor in a previous life. He certainly acted like someone with power, someone who was in control. But he also struck Hank as someone playing leader, kind of like a kid who got beat up a lot growing up, and now that he was an adult and a cop, he could push back at those who had wronged him as a kid. Hank knew the type, had even dealt with the very scenario.

Hank wanted to right hook him right there. He wanted to lay him out on the ground and put the butt of the rifle in his head. He wouldn't shoot him—too much noise, and noise was the last thing he wanted.

"Take a good look," Hank said. "And get to walking."

"But …"

"Look, you can stand here all day or all week. I don't care. But you must find Imeko—that is your only ticket back in. So stand around all you want. The sun is coming up, and Imeko has at least a day on us."

"He's an old man," Avis said. "He couldn't have gotten that far."

Hank whirled. This time he did punch Avis, hard and square in the left side of the jaw. Avis spun as he fell to the ground. Hank dropped onto his knees, letting the rifle fall from his hands. He grabbed Avis by the front of his shirt and pulled his face within inches of his, close enough to kiss if he wanted … or bite. And that is really what he wanted to do right then, wasn't it? To bite Avis and rip his skin away. He smelled the fear coursing through his blood, his heart pounding. He could smell the rich cigar aroma, and his mouth watered. Biting Avis is what he wanted.

That's what he feared, as well.

"He's an old man. That's exactly right. And you sent him out here. You knew he wouldn't last out here. And I swear, if we find him any way but alive, I will kill you."

Avis's eyes were huge. Hank could smell the fear pulsing through his blood better now. It made his own blood rush with something close to lust and hunger. His stomach grumbled, and his mouth was suddenly wet.

Hank shoved Avis hard into the concrete and stood. He shouldered the rifle and started away. He was breathing hard, and his head buzzed. He wiped his mouth with the back of one hand.

"Let's go."

He didn't look back to see if Avis was getting up and walking after him. He didn't care. He only wanted to find Imeko and find him alive. But deep down inside ... Hank pushed the thought away. He didn't want to think of Imeko dead.

Instead, he looked off in the distance, beyond the scorched buildings and the rotting city. Somewhere a billion miles away, the sun was rising. A brilliant yellow and purple line formed the horizon. There were dark clouds that would be white when the sun's light fully shone down on the world around them. For now, though, those clouds seemed ominous, as if the night knew the secrets of the dead; as if they hid all the lies every person had ever told, or maybe just the ones men like Harrison Avis had told.

He walked through the town, passed burned out cars and corpses with holes in their heads and flies buzzing around them, dipping in and out, snacking or laying eggs before flying off.

Occasionally, he saw a shambling biter on a side street or in one of the cars that hadn't been blown up when they converted the school into a safe zone. He thought to put them down but chose not to. Maybe Avis could do it. Or not.

Hank stopped and looked back. Avis followed about fifty feet away. He had picked up a pipe at some point and held it up, in the ready position just in case he needed to use it. Hank smiled.

At least he's thinking.

"Catch up," Hank said.

"Why should I?"

"Do you want to live to see tomorrow?"

Avis, as was his M.O., didn't answer. It was as if he were a defiant three-year-old who had gotten caught with his hand in the cookie jar and refused to admit he did anything wrong.

Hank, like a parent to a three-year-old, spoke calmly, but firm. "I know you are not used to answering questions, but that one is okay to answer."

Still, Avis said nothing.

Hank shrugged and shook his head. "Suit yourself. But when the biters come out, you'll want to be up here instead of back there. I won't see them behind me, but they will smell you coming a mile away. Keep that in mind."

"What do you mean they will smell me coming?"

"Catch up," Hank said, ignoring the question for the time being. He stopped in the middle of an intersection and looked in all four directions, including back at Avis, who had picked up his pace and closed the gap between them faster than Hank thought he would.

"What do you mean they will smell me coming?"

"They can see, for the most part, and hear somewhat, but not all that great. But they can smell. That is for certain. They can tell the difference between them and, well, you."

"What does that mean?"

Hank chuckled. It was comical how little this "leader" knew.

"It means they can smell the living, and they like the way the living smell and taste. You are a buffet for them, and let me tell you, once they latch onto you, it's all over but the turning."

"Turning?"

"Yeah. Turning."

119

"What ... what is that?"

"You don't know what that means?"

Avis started not to answer, but then shook his head. "No."

"How did you become the leader of an entire survival community and have no clue what is going on out here?"

"The power of persuasion, I guess. People want someone to follow. I just took the reigns and gave them a leader."

"Yeah, well, you're a crappy leader."

"I did the best I could, and I was doing just fine until you showed up."

"Yeah, I saw how you ran things—you're not a good person, no matter how much you tell yourself you are. You were a dictator, and one who would have led his people to their deaths before admitting he didn't know anything about the situation outside those walls."

"You're making me out to be a monster."

"You're not?"

"No. No, I'm not."

"You could have fooled me."

That ended the conversation as far as Hank was concerned. He searched the ground for any clues of an old man passing by. All he saw were the remains of some of the dead and garbage littering the roads. Buildings were missing windows and cars looked like they hadn't been moved in years. The early morning sun left eerie shadows between the buildings.

Hank started along a road, leaving Avis behind. If he wanted to catch up, he could, but as far as Hank knew, Imeko was still out there and every second he wasted with Avis a second closer to death Imeko came.

Maybe that's what he wants, a voice, one very much like Jeanette's, said in his head. He didn't bother looking around. He wouldn't see Jeanette, and if he did, he wouldn't be able to handle it.

"What if it is?" he asked as he passed a barbershop on the left. The red, white, and blue post in front of the shop was broken, leaving remnants of glass on the sidewalk. There were a couple of tipped over newspaper boxes in front. Not too far away, a dead man crawled along the road, both his feet missing, his pants shredded in places. Trailing behind him was a swath of brownish blood.

Then maybe you should let him go, Jeanette said softly.

"I can't do that, Babe. You know that."

Do I?

Hank walked up behind the struggling biter. It turned, looked at him through its cataract white eyes, and then continued his crawling. Hank remembered the day in the snow, when he wanted nothing more than to die. He ran out to the biters outside the house in Saluda. Getting their attention was easy. Keeping it was another matter. They turned from him and stumbled away, even as he held his arms out, begging them to kill him. He lost his mind that day and bashed the dead's head in before collapsing to the ground. The snow melted around him from the heat spilling from his body due to the high fever.

The dead had walked away that time. This time the dead just crawled away as if it never saw Hank.

Hank looked back. Avis wasn't too far from him, but he had stopped. He stared down at the crawling corpse not far from Hank.

"Is that …?"

"A biter?" Hank asked. "Absolutely."

"Are you going to kill it?" Avis's voice was shaky. He held the pipe close, as if he were hugging it. To Hank it looked like Avis treated the pole like a security blanket. He thought of Linus from the old Peanuts cartoons and how he had a security blanket.

Always holding tight to it, he thought.

"No," Hank said.

"Why not? It's a biter."

"You want it dead? You kill it."

"What? Me?"

"Yeah. You. Come on. You need to learn something really quick about these guys. They might be slow, but they are relentless. They keep coming and coming and coming until you either put them down or they kill you."

Avis didn't get any closer to the crawling biter. He only stared at it, the pipe snugged tight to his chest.

"Come on, Avis. Smash its head."

He shook his head. "I don't want to."

"I'm not asking you to. I'm telling you get over here."

"But ..."

"Now!" Hank yelled.

Avis flinched. Hank liked having the roles reversed here. He liked being the intimidating one, even if he wasn't really trying to be. The biter turned its body toward Hank. It gnashed its teeth in their direction.

"Walker, I'm not getting near that thing."

Hank walked over to Avis. "Remember what I said about these biters. They were once people. Living and breathing with emotions and fears and everything else a person is. It is not a thing. It is a person. It might be dead, but up here ..." Hank tapped the side of his head, "... they are still very much alive. Now get over here and smash its head with your pipe and end this man's suffering."

"Suffering?" Avis almost laughed the word. "You think he is suffering? That thing is dead, and it is mindless and ..."

Avis screamed and stumbled backward. He tripped when his heel hit the base of the sidewalk. Then he fell, his butt striking concrete, the pipe clanging loudly and rolling a couple feet from him. He tried to back away, but from the looks of the way he moved, he was in pain.

Hank turned and saw several biters bumbling toward them. He didn't take the time to count.

Instead, he braced himself for their attack. He raised the weapon, knowing full well, if he flipped the safety off, he could take them down quickly. Hank didn't do that. Hank backed up, putting very little distance between him and the dead as he led them to Avis.

"What are you doing?" Avis screamed.

"Get up and fight for your life or lay there and get ripped apart by that small group of biters. I don't care which one."

Hank walked by Avis, leaving him on the sidewalk, scrambling backwards.

"Walker!" Avis yelled. "Walker! Don't leave me here like this!"

Hank did as Avis had so many times—he said nothing. He leaned against the wall of the barber shop and folded his hands over his chest.

Avis reached the wall Hank leaned against. He pushed himself onto his feet and turned to Hank. "Are you crazy?"

"Maybe," Hank said. That was the truth. Hank thought he might just be nuts. He left the safety of a compound, partially because he hadn't cooperated, and it put him in a situation where he had to oust this blowhard next to him.

125

"You have a gun! Kill them!"

"Get your pipe, Avis. They'll be here in a minute or so."

"You're serious?"

"Dead serious."

"But …"

Again, Hank grabbed Avis by the shirt, but instead of pulling him so they were face to face, he shoved him toward the biters. He stumbled into the road, almost fell, but managed to keep his balance. He plucked the pipe from the ground and held it in both hands.

"You ever play baseball, Avis?"

Avis shot him a glance and looked back at the five dead men coming for him. Groans tore from their throats and they reached out with boney hands missing most of the flesh from the tips.

"You know how to swing a bat, right?"

"Of course I do," Avis yelled back. He was now slightly crouched, and the pipe was over his shoulder. It wasn't the best way to hold a bat, but it would do in a pinch, and boy was this a pinch he was in.

Avis swung the pipe at the first one—a young man with most of his hair gone, his face sagging off

126

his skull. His clothes were blood-stained and hung off his body. His mouth slackened. He moaned as one hand reached for Avis. His head whipped to the side as the pipe struck him in the face. His jaw snapped, sending it sideways and tearing the skin away. The biter fell to the ground. There was a loud pop as his elbow broke. He tried to stand.

"You have to smash his skull, not his face," Hank yelled. He pushed off the wall and swung the rifle off his shoulder. He put the butt of the gun to his shoulder and hoped the kickback wouldn't break his collar bone the way Ox had broken Lee's all those years ago when they were kids.

Avis raised the pipe over his head and brought it down on Broke Jaw's head. The hollow crack and pop that came from him clearly made Avis cringe. He backed away shaking his head in what Hank took as complete shock.

Hank squeezed off one shot, taking out the biter closest to Avis. He did the same to the others, one bullet, one kill, each one sheering off the top of the biters' heads, leaving only the crawler moving.

Avis dropped the pipe. Like minutes earlier, his heel hit the sidewalk. Unlike that incident, he didn't fall on his behind. He simply put his other foot onto the sidewalk and backed up to the wall of the barbershop where he stopped.

"The first kill is always the hardest."

Avis turned his face to Hank. His eyes held the shock of someone who had just been in a car accident and everyone died except for him. Hank supposed this is exactly what had happened. There may not have been an accident, but there was a wreck of bodies only a few feet from them, one of which Avis had managed to bash in the head.

"You got one more," Hank said and nodded toward the crawler. It had managed to turn itself around and was coming toward them, one shredded hand at a time.

Avis looked at the crawler. "Seriously?"

"Yeah, I'm serious."

Avis pushed off the wall and took a few staggering steps toward the pipe in the road. He looked like a man who had worked a long day and was too exhausted to really go much further. He knelt, keeping his eyes on the crawler, and felt around for the pipe. His hand found it and the fingers wrapped around it. Avis stood upright and took another few steps. His left foot struck one of the forever dead, and he stumbled a little. He didn't fall; he appeared to be in a fog.

Avis reached the crawler and lifted his arms above his head. A scream left his throat as he brought the pipe down onto the crawler's skull. It ruptured like an overripe melon. Avis lifted his arms again and brought the pipe down several more times, bashing the crawler's head until the skull was a pulpy, bloody mess.

He tossed the pipe away and fell back to the ground. Avis either laughed or cried. Hank couldn't tell, but he thought it might have been a little bit of both. The sound that came from his mouth was much like a donkey's bray, complete with deep breaths before each one. His face turned purple. For a fleeting second, Hank grew concerned for Avis. The moment passed as Hank remembered Avis had sent others out here, more than likely, to their deaths.

Hank shouldered the rifle. Then he thought to check to see how many bullets were left. It turned out, there were none. He shook his head—just enough, he thought—and set the gun against the barbershop wall. If anyone was to come along and see it, they might think it was set there by an unwitting individual who either died not long after or who was still around, watching to see if anyone would try to take it.

Hank walked off. At some point, he would need to look for another weapon. For now, he had his knife and Avis had his pipe. Then he stopped and looked back at the gun as Avis continued to donkey laugh (or cry) next to the crawler. It did look like someone had just left it there and forgotten it. Hank went back, picked it up, and shouldered it. It might be empty, but Avis didn't know, and Hank had a feeling he was going to need it for perception purposes.

Hank gave the waning, donkey braying Avis a nudge with his foot. "Come on," he said and walked off.

Avis could stay there for all he cared, his mind cracking. He could be biter food, and it would be fine with Hank. But he felt the need to be courteous enough to let him know he was moving on.

He made his way through the streets, eventually coming to an overpass. Though the sun had come out and the world was cast in a yellow hue, beneath the overpass was dark. He couldn't tell if there were any biters beneath it … or any crazies.

He stopped at the edge of it, searched the dark for any movement and saw none.

"Where are we going?" Avis asked from behind him. His voice was distant—nothing like the cocky, self-assured leader of the survivor camp. He certainly didn't sound like the man who had tried to intimidate Hank into telling him stuff that was none of his business.

Hank looked back. Avis stood, empty-handed. He had left the pipe behind. He was no longer laugh-crying, but his face was clearly streaked with the remnants of tears. There was plenty of blood drying on his shirt. The shock that in his eyes from earlier was mostly gone, but Hank thought he might never get over what he had experienced.

How safe does that make you? he asked himself.

"I don't know," Hank said.

"Are we still looking for the Indian?"

Hank wanted to spin on him, maybe knock him down. *The Indian* seemed degrading to Hank. Instead he simply said, "Yes," and made his way beneath the overpass. If there were biters in there and if Avis followed, Hank had a feeling they would go for the newly de-virgined biter killer.

A bottle skidded away when his foot hit it, coming to a stop and shattering when it hit one of the pillars. Hank didn't stop and didn't look back to see if Avis was following or still standing at the mouth of the overpass. When he reached the other end, he finally stopped just before stepping into the sunlight. Off to his right was a white, five-gallon paint bucket, and two cinder blocks—each one opposite the other, as if they had been chairs and the bucket had been a table.

In his mind he could see two people sitting opposite each other playing blackjack or poker or even WAR (but not Go Fish). He imagined they were probably both homeless and the deck of cards had been dirty, the edges rounded from years of use. There were probably a few creases in some cards. An old green rubber band, like the ones used to hold newspapers together, probably kept the cards together. But something told him that wasn't quite right.

Maybe it was checkers, he thought. It didn't matter. That world was over. That world was dead. More than likely whoever sat on the bucket was also dead, and maybe among those who were now biters. *Maybe they're still alive.* He doubted it, but part of him held out hope they were. And if not, maybe they would cross paths and Hank could put them down.

Hank left the darkness of the overpass and no biters had come after him. The road opened before him. He looked both ways as if checking for cars, just as Mom would have told him to. Hank turned left. Out the corner of one eye he saw Avis. Hank glanced back at him. In the distance, close to the mouth of the other end of the overpass staggered a biter. Hank couldn't make out what he looked like from a distance, but he knew it was following them. It might catch up. It might not.

Hank walked on, following the road, passing houses in a neck of the town that wasn't burned and rotting away. It wasn't the nicest of neighborhoods. The rich certainly never lived here. Some houses were rundown and probably had been before the end of the world. Many of the cars in driveways were older models—nothing within the last five or six years. He continued, leaving the rundown neighborhood.

Behind him came Avis, still no weapon in hand. Behind him, the biter from beneath the overpass followed, along with three of his friends.

Another block down and no sign of Imeko. Hank came to the end of another road and saw the cemetery off in the distance. Though he wasn't sure why, he suddenly felt very drawn to it. Fear swept over him. It was something so certain he couldn't ignore it. Hank started jogging and then broke into a full-on run just seconds later.

He reached the gate, winded. His hands went to his knees, and he took several deep breaths. He stood straight and put his hands behind his head.

Breathe, Hank. Breathe.

Hank caught a sight in the cemetery that would have made his blood run cold before being bitten. It was a sight that would surely make Avis turn and run.

Deep in the cemetery were a dozen or more biters. They all seemed to mingle around the same set of graves, as if a funeral had just been held for a loved one and they were about to plant the person in the ground. The only thing missing was the preacher at the front of the group and the tarp with the name of the funeral home in charge of the burial above a newly dug grave.

Hank took a step into the cemetery, trying to be as quiet as possible. He didn't believe he needed to be silent, but he also didn't know for certain if the dead couldn't smell him or sense him. Why take a chance? A few more steps in and he noticed a shovel lying on the ground, the spade end bloodied. A biter lay dead near it, its head caved in. Hank picked up the shovel and held it over his shoulder, ready to swing if needed.

A few more steps in and he stopped cold. The biters turned, their cloudy eyes looking toward him. Their mouths and chins, and the fronts of shirts and blouses, were soaked in blood. Their hands were coated in slick scarlet. The first of them took an unsteady step forward. Then another. And another.

The rest followed, moans escaping their throats. A little girl fell, her head smacking one of the headstones. Hank wanted to close his eyes. He wanted to be anywhere but there. But closing his eyes would mean seeing the little girl at the lake, the one screaming for help; the one who, more than likely, had seen him and Hetch outside of the house where Hetch's friend had died and been put down; the one who Hank had run through the yards to save; the one who took a bullet to the head and crumpled to the ground, her feet going out from beneath her. He shook his head, not because of the dead who drew closer to him, but because he would never be able to get the little girl out of his mind, the image of her, first living and running and screaming, next with the bullet in her head, blood spraying out from the wound, both in the front and back of her skull, and finally as a mutilated corpse the biters had decided to snack on, even after she had died.

Hank blinked several times, suddenly aware at how close the dead were to him. He began to back away, then stopped. They weren't looking at him or even walking toward him. Hank lifted the shovel back over his shoulder, ready to swing if needed. The first of the biters—an average looking, middle-aged man who had been balding before death claimed him—veered to Hank's right, his mouth open, the one eye he still had focused somewhere else besides him.

Hetch and Walmart came to mind, how he had said the dead didn't seem to notice him. It was crazy to think of then. Even crazier now as the second and third and the next half dozen biters went by him without even looking in his direction. Still, Hank held the shovel high, ready to swing.

His muscles were tense, his blood rushing through his veins, heat ran along his face, ears and neck.

Then his arms dropped. The shovel didn't quite fall from his hands, but he didn't exactly hold it tight any longer. Lying on the ground where the biters had been having their funeral service lay Imeko. He had no shirt and his stomach had been torn open. Both arms held bite marks in some places and were missing bits of flesh in others. The skin on the right side of his face had been either bitten off or ripped off by the bony hands of one of the biters.

From the looks of him he hadn't been dead too long.

"No." His voice felt so small, as if it came from a long distance away. He heard it, but he could hardly believe it was his. He could also hardly believe the mess Imeko was, lying half on his back and half on his side, his legs crossed at the ankles as if he had been resting peacefully instead of dead and munched on by a bunch of biters.

The real shock came a few seconds after the last of the biters had passed him, and Avis had started to yell for Hank's help. He was aware someone needed him, but Avis was the furthest person from

137

his mind. He watched, for how long he didn't know. The yelling was still there, but it was like the sound of a buzzing fly in his ear. It was annoying, nothing more at the moment.

Then it happened. The pinky on Imeko's right hand twitched. It wasn't much, and if he hadn't been looking for it he would have missed it. His hand jerked, the fingers suddenly squeezing into a fist, and then released, as if Imeko flexed his hand. The arm jerked, and then it spasmed to the point where it looked like it was flopping. His body convulsed, and he flipped completely onto his back, then rolled onto his stomach.

Imeko got his hands underneath him and pushed himself onto his knees. He struggled but managed to stand.

"No," Hank said again, his voice cracking.

Imeko was unsteady. He turned in a circle as if testing out his legs, then he faced Hank. Blood fell from the ripped flap on his cheek. His intestines hung down between his legs, like a gray rope.

"No."

The yell for help pulled him from the grotesque thing Imeko had turned into. Hank looked back. Avis stood on one of the tombs. It was cracked in one corner. He kicked at the dead as they reached for him.

"Help me," Avis screamed and kicked a female biter in the face. Her head snapped backward. She began to fall, but before she could hit the ground, another two biters had pushed up against the tomb, pinning her upper torso against the rectangular granite box.

Avis screamed again as a hand brushed against his leg, and he almost pitched head over heels off the tomb and into the waiting hands and mouths of the dead surrounding him. He looked at Hank, terror in his eyes.

Hank grabbed the shovel in both hands and ran for the tomb. He swung the shovel at the back of the head of the one nearest him. The biter's head shot forward, his arms going out to his side, his momentum driving him into some of the other biters. Hank yelled as he swung the shovel again. The spade clanked hard on the back of one of the biters' heads. He didn't wait for it to fall to the side before he swung again and again and again. As the biters fell, Hank swung. He was aware he was screaming louder than Avis was. As his arms grew heavy, he swung the spade at the biters' legs, taking them down and smashing their skulls with either his bootheel or the shovel.

By the time Hank had taken down the last of the biters—an elderly woman with faded blue hair, greenish gray skin, and one tooth in her mouth—he was exhausted. He dropped the shovel and looked at the carnage around him. Sixteen biters were finally dead, their souls released from the walking corpses they had turned into.

Avis stood on the tomb, panting. His eyes were no longer wide orbs set in deep sockets but weakened and barely open. Sweat and blood spilled down his face.

"Thank you," he said and put a hand out for Hank to help him down.

Hank shook his head. "Don't thank me," he growled through gasps for breaths.

"What? I don't under—"

Hank reached up and grabbed Avis's arm. He gave a strong pull and Avis fell forward. He screamed as his feet left the top of the tomb. He screamed even louder when he landed on the ground, his elbow taking the brunt of the weight and snapping like a brittle stick. The bone shoved right through the muscle and skin, jutting out about four inches. Another scream came from Avis. He rolled over, the hand of his non-broken arm shaking as he stared at the bone jutting from his arm, his mouth open wide, the scream seeming to go on far longer than anyone should have breath.

Hank watched as the blood flowed from the wound and splashed onto the ground. He could smell the rich, coppery smell of adrenaline in the blood. The scream faded from his ears, and he was suddenly walking *(lurching)* forward. He dropped to his knees, Avis seemingly not noticing him as his eyes held on the wounded arm. Hank heard Avis's heart pumping the blood through his body and pushing a little bit more out of the gash where the bone jutted.

Then Hank did something that would forever change his life. He looked at Avis, his mouth still open, the scream somehow still coming from his throat, his eyes unbelievably large. Without thought given, Hank bent over and sunk his teeth into Avis's arm. There was no resistance from Avis as he jerked his head sideways, tearing the flesh, but not pulling it free. Hank yanked his head in the other direction, the meat in his mouth ripping away from Avis's arm.

The punch came to his right shoulder, and Hank rolled away from Avis onto his side and then onto his knees. He chewed the flesh in his mouth. It was much like raw steak—pink and bloody and somewhat disgusting in his opinion. But he couldn't stop chewing, and when a piece of the flesh came free from the larger mass, he swallowed it down.

Hank continued to chew as Imeko hobbled forward, his mutilated corpse wobbling from side to side with each step he took. He didn't moan, he didn't extend his arms out, and he never once looked toward Hank. Like Hank a minute earlier, Imeko dropped to his knees, but he didn't bite Avis in the wounded arm. He went for the throat, one that, until Imeko sank his teeth into it, was still screaming for all it was worth.

Hank saw all this, including the blood gushing from Avis's throat when Imeko pulled his head back, his mouth full of tender meat. For Hank, it didn't matter what happened to Avis (he would have killed him anyway), or that Imeko leaned in and took another pound of flesh from the now dead Harrison Avis. What mattered is his stomach grumbled and rumbled, and the taste of blood in his mouth made him want to throw up, but it also made him want to crawl back to Avis and take another bite. He wanted to place his lips on the open wound at his arm and suckle blood like a baby to a woman's breast. But unlike the need to feed to survive, Hank knew his feeding would be blood lust at its finest.

He dropped onto his bottom and scooted away. Tears had formed in his eyes at the sad realization, one far worse than seeing Imeko dead and feasting on Avis. He shook his head violently several times as he continued to move further from the two dead men. Eventually, his back struck a tombstone, and he came to a stop. He looked on for several long minutes. Then he wiped his mouth and looked at the smear of blood on his arm and hand.

Hank Walker cried. It was hard and ugly and filled with snot bubbles. His vision grew blurry, but he could still see Imeko on his knees. He could still hear the rending of flesh from bone and the steady smacking of lips as Imeko chewed chunks of Avis's flesh.

It took him a while to gain control of himself. When he did, he was drained of almost all his energy. He stood with the help of the tombstone.

One glance at it told him the woman buried there was named Susanna, and she had died very young—twenty-three. He couldn't read much else on the headstone. Most of it had eroded over time.

His legs were weak as he walked over to Imeko. He slid his knife from his back pocket and flicked the blade open with two fingers and a snap of his wrist.

"I'm sorry," Hank said and drove the blade as far as he could into Imeko's temple. The old man's body collapsed onto his meal. Hank didn't bother to pull the blade free. He just let it slide from his hand.

He turned and went back to where the remains of the biters lay. Shovel in hand he walked through the cemetery, searching for a spot to dig a hole. He found one and began digging.

It would be mid-afternoon before he finished with the hole and had Imeko in his arms. He carried him to the hole. Then he spent the next hour shoveling dirt into the grave. Several biters passed the graveyard's entrance. They didn't seem to notice Hank as he buried Imeko. One woman, who was bent over at the midsection, her back eternally twisted, took a few steps into the graveyard. If she had been alive, she wouldn't have been able to move much at all. She looked around and seemed to smell the air around her. Possibly satisfied there was no food there, she ambled on, her neck craned up so she could see where she was going.

If she can even see, Hank thought.

Hank went back to burying Imeko. When he was finished, he tamped the dirt with the flat side of the shovel. He drove the spade into the soft dirt. It would serve as a marker, at least until someone else came along who needed it. How long that would be, Hank didn't quite know. It could be tomorrow. It could be never. He was banking on the never.

Hank took a deep breath and released it. He felt like a balloon when the air is let out. Pretty soon he would be nothing but skin on the ground, his breath gone, his body deflated. He turned to leave, to head … head where?

Before he could think on the question too long, he heard a gurgled moan that could have been the growl of a dying dog. He spun around, expecting to see a mongrel standing there, froth coming from its mouth, its body nothing more than fur and bones to the point its ribs could be seen. The dog would be hungry and probably wouldn't care if Hank was alive or dead or undead.

What he saw wasn't a starving dog, but Harrison Avis trying to sit up. He tried to push up with his broken arm and fell back to the ground. The groans from him sounded like Avis was in more pain than he had ever been in.

"How you doing, Avis?"

A moan came from the dead man.

"Yeah. I know. It sucks."

Avis's eyes hadn't filmed over yet, but soon they would. Hank could see the fading blue in them. He could also see Avis's soul begging Hank to free him.

Hank looked away and down at the ground. He shuffled his feet. "I … I didn't mean to take a bite out of you." Hank meant this. He truly felt bad, but not for Avis. For himself. Even if no one else found out about what happened here, he would know, and he wouldn't be able to trust himself around people—at least living people.

Avis's groan sounded like a frustrated yelp as he fell back again.

146

"Good luck getting up," Hank said and turned to leave. He reached cemetery gate and stopped. What if Avis managed to get up? Would he remembered where the survivor camp was? What if a living person came upon him? What if he killed a living person? What if the person was Bobby or Jake or Hetch?

It doesn't matter who it is. Bobby. Jake. Hetch. Some random stranger. If I don't put him down and he kills someone, that's on me.

Hank turned around to see Avis on his side, his busted arm useless, and his brain so much mush he couldn't seem to figure out he could use his other arm to get up. He weaved through the graves, passing Susanna's final resting place along the wall where a tree had grown tall over the years, its branches casting shade beneath it. He reached for the shovel he had used to kill all the biters around the tomb Avis had stood on, and then stopped. He looked around the boneyard, squinting as he did so, until his eyes fell on the broken headstone not too far away from where he stood.

It was only two dozen or so steps to the grave where the broken stone lay. Hank knelt. With both hands, he hefted a piece of the stone from the ground. On it was engraved the name Clements. He thought it was a last name, but it could have been a first name, depending on when the person beneath the ground there had lived. The stone was heavy, but not so much he couldn't carry it and put it over his head when the time came.

That time was half a minute later as he stood over Harrison Avis's struggling half-dead corpse.

"This is all your fault," he said and lifted the stone above his head. He slung it down as hard as he could. It struck Avis's head with such force it drove it down into the grassy ground. His head ruptured, and blood and gore splattered the ground and Hank's shoes and pant legs.

Hank stared at Avis's body for a minute, maybe two, but no more. Then, as he had done moments earlier, he turned to leave the cemetery. He passed Clements's grave (first or last name he would never know) and muttered, "Sorry about the headstone," as he passed it.

He reached the gate and looked to his left, back toward the survivor camp. He shook his head. Even as he felt his heart rip, he knew what he had to do, if not for his own good, then for what remained of his family's.

"I can't go back," he said, solidifying the truth in his mind.

He made a right out of the cemetery. Ahead was the broke back woman, her neck craned upward. Lying on the ground was a red brick—one that had been part of the fence at one time. He picked it up and followed the woman.

AJB

Dear Faithful Readers,

When I wrote what would become the first chapter of *Dredging Up Memories*, I had no intentions of writing any further. I had been challenged to write a zombie story with emotions. It was my attempt to prove to another writer—a very critical one, whom I respect but sometimes despised his thoughts on the way things should be—that a zombie story wasn't just about walking corpses tearing people apart and eating them.

On a whim, I sent the story to a website called *Tales of the Zombie Wars*. To my surprise, they picked it up, and a couple months later, it appeared on their website. This was one of those sites that allow people to comment on content. I was surprised to see all the positive comments about that short piece. One of those comments read as follows:

"I like the story very much. It really finds a balance between having a John Wayne who shoots at everything without mercy and a total coward who starts crying for anything as a main character. I'm only somewhat missing a closing to the story. Wouldn't surprise (or disappoint) me to see this story continue ..."

Up to that point, I had no intentions of writing further about Hank Walker. It was supposed to be a one-off story. After all, zombies weren't really my thing. Then came that comment, that statement. One thing I know about writing is when something looks like it could work, run with it. I wrote another chapter. And another. And another. Each one went on the *Tales of the Zombie Wars* website, and each one garnered quite a few comments.

It is that one story, that challenge made to me, that set into motion *Dredging Up Memories*. After that novel came out, I packed away Hank Walker and Humphrey and all the other characters who survived the zombie apocalypse, with no intention of writing about them again.

Then the reviews started coming in. Most of them were positive. and the negative ones really weren't bad. The next thing I knew one question was being asked: *will there be a sequel?*

The short answer was no. The long answer was let me think about it, sleep on it, and we'll see.

Then one evening about six months after *Dredging Up Memories* was released, the idea for *Interrogations* came to me. What has Hank Walker gotten himself into? Sure, he survived being bitten and somehow found his brother and son. But just what type of problems could he face in a safe haven? Well, someone had to run that place, right? It was a small thought, just an inkling, but as it marinated in that sauce called Creativity, it grew arms and legs and a head and mouth. Then it started to speak.

As it spoke to me, it started reminding me Hank had been bitten. Though he had been 'cured' by the water of Healing Springs, was he truly healed? Or is there an after effect to the virus that claimed millions of lives?

It took longer than I thought it would to write, but when I was finished, I was happy with the results. I was happy with where I took Hank and the storyline. I was happy with how I ended it. However, that ending presented another problem. It was open ended and that means there could possibly be another novella or novel in this story arc.

Will there be? Hank is still talking, still walking, still killing biters. Take it for what it is.

If you've read this far, I thank you for taking the time to come along with me on this journey. As always, until we meet again, my friends, be kind to one another.

A.J.

The Little Page of Thanks

Most writers spend hours creating their stories, usually alone. However, there are those who have a helping hand in the finished product. In no particular order, I would like to thank:

My wife, Cate. Y'all might get tired of seeing her name in this section, but without her, there would be no stories. So, y'all can thank her, too.

Larissa Bennett and Tara Bennett. Over the last couple of years, these two ladies have become like family. Larissa, who is my editor, made *Interrogations* shine. Tara proofed the story, going behind both myself and Larissa to make sure it is at its best.

Lisa Vasquez, the owner of *Stitched Smile Publications*, who has been my publisher for the last three or so years. Like Larissa and Tara, she has become family and co-conspirator over the last several years.

Finally, You, my Faithful Readers. Enough said.

About the Author

A.J. Brown is a southern-born writer who tells emotionally charged, character driven stories that often delve into the darker parts of the human psyche. Most of his stories have the southern country feel of his childhood.

A.J. writes in a conversational style that draws the reader in and holds their attention. His characters are average people with average lives who are layered with memories and emotions and are fallible, just like anyone else.

He adheres to the philosophy that everything in life is a story.

Though he writes mostly darker stories, he does so without unnecessary gore, coarse language, or sex.

A.J. is also a husband to Cate and a father to two kids, referred to as The Girl and The Boy, and who often inspire him in the most interesting ways.

More than 200 of his stories have been published in various online and print publications. His story, *Mother Weeps*, was nominated for a Pushcart Award in 2010. His story, *Picket Fences*, was the editor's choice story for Necrotic Tissue in October of 2010. The story, *Numbers*, won the quarterly contest at WilyWriters.com in June of 2013.

His novel, *Dredging Up Memories,* was released in May of 2016. John Malone, the narrator of the audiobook won the *Voice Arts Award* for best voice over in a science fiction narration in December of 2107.

You can purchase all of his books, including *Dredging Up Memories*, *Voices*, *A Stitch of Madness*, and *Interrogations* (all released by Stitched Smile Publications), or any of his other works—*Along the Splintered Path*, *Southern Bones*, *Cory's Way*, *Ball Four*, *The Forgetful Man's Disease*, *Beautiful Minds*, and *Zombie*, his nonfiction novella, *Closing the Wound*, and his collaborative effort with M.F. Wahl, *All We See is the End*, on Amazon.

A list of his publications along with links to many of his stories can be found on his blog, *Type AJ Negative*

You can find A.J. at these places:

Type AJ Negative (BLOG):
https://typeajnegative.wordpress.com

Amazon Author Page: https://www.amazon.com/A.-J.-Brown/e/B006UN58R6/ref=dp_byline_cont_ebooks_1

A.J. Brown Facebook Fan Page:
https://www.facebook.com/typeajnegative/

Twitter: @ajbrown36

Instagram: ajbrownstoryteller

email: <u>1horrorwithheart@gmail.com</u>